KRISTY + BART = ?

Other books by
Ann M. Martin

Rachel Parker, Kindergarten Show-off
Eleven Kids, One Summer
Ma and Pa Dracula
Yours Turly, Shirley
Ten Kids, No Pets
Slam Book
Just a Summer Romance
Missing Since Monday
With You and Without You
Me and Katie (the Pest)
Stage Fright
Inside Out
Bummer Summer

BABY-SITTERS LITTLE SISTER series
THE BABY-SITTERS CLUB mysteries
THE BABY-SITTERS CLUB series

KRISTY + BART = ?

Ann M. Martin

AN
APPLE
PAPERBACK

SCHOLASTIC INC.
New York Toronto London Auckland Sydney

The author gratefully acknowledges
Peter Lerangis
for his help in
preparing this manuscript

Cover art by Hodges Soileau

ISBN 0-590-22879-X

12 11 10 9 8 7 6 5 4 3 2 1   6 7 8 9/9 0 1/0

Printed in the U.S.A.   40

First Scholastic printing, March 1996

CHAPTER 1

"Ugh," groaned Stacey McGill.

"Oh, no," Jessica Ramsey added.

"Not again," Mary Anne Spier complained.

Claudia Kishi shook her head. "I can't take it anymore."

Grimly I stared out the front door of Stoneybrook Middle School. It was snowing. Thick, swirling snow, already deep enough to show footprints.

"Guys," I said with a heavy sigh, "we'll just have to deal with this."

We all trudged outside.

Call me Ebenezer. Ebenezer Scrooge Thomas. Or maybe Kristy the Grinch. I'm sorry, but I was not in the mood for snow. As you can tell, neither were my friends.

Back in December, I couldn't wait for winter. The first snowstorm was great. So were the second, third, and fourth. Then came the ice storm in January. Then a few more snows. By mid-February, my arms were tired from shoveling, my boots were starting to smell, and the snow on the sidewalk had turned an interesting shade of gray-brown.

Now it was March. We'd had a whole week of warm, springlike weather. My down coat was at the cleaners, and I was already thinking about softball season.

And flowers.

And spring vacation.

But did the weather cooperate? Noooo. Here we were, two and a half weeks from spring, caught in a blizzard.

It just didn't seem fair.

Outside, the snow soaked up the bus engine noise like a gigantic muffler. We huddled together against the wind. The flakes seemed to be shooting upward from the sidewalk.

"In like a lion, huh?" Abby Stevenson said.

"Brrrr." Claudia shivered. "Very leonine."

"*Leonine?*" I repeated.

"It means, 'like a lion,' " Claudia explained.

"How do you know that?" asked Stacey.

Claudia raised her eyebrows. "I'm not as stupid as I look."

"Uh, g-g-guys," said Mallory Pike through chattering teeth, "can we c-c-continue this another t-t-time?"

"Yeah, I'm feeling kind of . . . you know, *icicline*," Abby said. "See you all later."

She ran toward the bus.

" 'Like an icicle,' " Stacey explained.

Claudia shot her a Look. "Thank you."

" 'Bye!" I shouted, running after Abby.

Riding the bus is not exactly my favorite thing to do, but that day I felt pretty lucky. Inside it was so nice and warm, I didn't even notice the pukey green color of the walls and ceiling.

Of all my closest friends, only Abby and her twin sister live bus-distance from school. Our neighborhood is in the countryish section of Stoneybrook, Connecticut. Some people call it the rich section. I don't, because that would make me sound snobby.

And I, Kristy Thomas, am the exact opposite of a snob. I'm also hard-working, cheerful, lovable, fair, and very take-charge. Oh, and modest, too. (Please don't barf, I'm just stating facts.)

More facts: I'm thirteen years old. I'm in the eighth grade at Stoneybrook Middle School. I have shoulder-length brown hair and dark-brown eyes. I'm five feet tall and I dress casually all the time.

I live in a huge house, sort of a mansion, because my stepdad is a millionaire. My family is highly blended. (Don't you love that word? It makes us sound like a big banana milkshake.) Actually, it means my mom and stepdad each had families before they married each other. The Thomas part of the blend includes my mom, my three brothers (Charlie's seventeen, Sam's fifteen, and David Michael's seven and a half), and my grandmother, Nannie. Nannie moved in with us to help take care of Emily Michelle, my adopted sister who was born in Vietnam. My stepdad, Watson Brewer, has a seven-year-old daughter (Karen) and a four-year-old son (Andrew) who live with us every other month. Our pets are Boo-Boo the cat, Shannon the puppy, and two goldfish named Crystal Light the Second and Goldfishie. Whenever Karen and Andrew arrive, they bring Emily Junior the rat and Bob the hermit crab.

Got all that? Good, because I'll be giving you a quiz later on.

Just joking.

Okay, I might as well say it right now. I do have a sense of humor. Despite what my friends might tell you. They'll say I'm loud, bossy, and opinionated.

Hard to believe, I know. First of all, I'm only opinionated when I know I'm right. Maybe I go overboard, but I can't help it. I'm a real solutions person. If I see a problem, *boooinnng*, my mind springs into action. When others are still in the head-scratching stage, I already have an answer. My friends call me the Idea Machine.

How did I become like this? Practice. My family may be comfortable now, but life used to be full of problems. When I was a little kid, right after David Michael was born, my dad abandoned our family. Mom had a lot to handle, and I thought of all kinds of ways to help out.

One of my all-time best ideas, the Baby-sitters Club, occurred to me one day when Mom had trouble finding a sitter for David Michael. My solution was simple: a group of reliable sitters who meet regularly to take phone calls and assign jobs. Not only did it help my mom, but it changed forever the lives of many Stoneybrook parents.

Thank you, thank you. Don't applaud, just send clients. (Kidding!)

As for being bossy, well, I have to be. I'm club president. I have to be loud, too. Come to a meeting someday and you'll know why.

Now that we've got all that straight, back to the bus on that frozen March afternoon.

Abby had already found a seat and was gabbing away. I walked to the back of the bus to sit next to her twin sister, Anna.

Abby and Anna are my newest friends. They moved to Stoneybrook from Long Island.

Their mom works in New York City, for a publishing company. (I know their dad died a few years ago in a car accident, but they haven't spoken much about him.) They're identical twins, technically. But boy, are they different. Abby's kind of goofy and loud, not too studious, and pretty athletic. Her hair is dark brown and bouncy, she has asthma, and she's allergic to about five million things. Anna's quiet and thoughtful and a really talented musician (she's played violin in a professional orchestra). Her hair is shorter than Abby's, she doesn't care about sports, and she hasn't the slightest trace of an allergy.

Both of them, by the way, are going to become Bat Mitzvahs next month. That's a rite of passage for most thirteen-year-old Jewish girls. It means they have to lead part of a Shabbat service and read from the holiest book in their religion, the Torah. It also means they have to study like crazy (the reading is in Hebrew).

That day on the bus, however, Anna was deeply involved in a book that appeared to be written in English.

"Hey, don't you have orchestra on Tuesdays?" I asked.

"Huh?" Anna looked up with a start. (I guess I should have said hello first.) "Oh, hi. Mrs. Pinelli canceled rehearsal. She wanted to drive right home because of the weather."

"Disgusting day, huh?" I said.

A smile crept across Anna's face as she looked out the window. "Oh, I don't know. I think it's kind of beautiful."

"Yeah. It is. I mean, the way it looks and all. It's just that we've had so much of it. That's the disgusting part."

Anna nodded. Then she started reading again.

I took a closer look at her book. The words *The Infinite Variety of Music* were printed across the top of one page.

"Is that good?" I asked.

"Mm-hm." Anna glanced up briefly. "Leonard Bernstein was so brilliant."

"Yeah," I said, nodding in agreement.

Right. Did I know who Leonard Bernstein was? No way. I guess he was a musician (*duh*).

I like Anna, but honestly, sometimes when I'm with her I feel like a doofus.

Personally, I don't know a French horn from an English muffin. But ask me who the top ten batters in the National and American leagues were last year, and I'll rattle them off. I love sports. Did I tell you I happen to be the founder, manager, and head coach of a softball team? It's called Kristy's Krushers, and it's for kids who aren't quite ready for Little League.

As the bus rolled slowly away from the

school, I waved to Claudia, Mary Anne, Mallory, Jessi, and Stacey, who were slogging home in the snow. I felt bad for them.

Then Anna started chatting about Beethoven and Brahms and Leonard Bernstein, and I felt bad for me.

I guess life is a trade-off.

By the time I arrived home, the snow had tapered off and the sun was breaking through the clouds. Snowplows had already cleared the street, and kids were jumping into the piled-up snow. A snowball fight was in full force at the home of my neighbors, the Papadakises. I had to admit, McLelland Road looked like a beautiful winter postcard.

I said good-bye to Abby and Anna, then walked up my driveway between a set of fresh tire tracks. I figured my brother Charlie had just driven home from school in the Junk Bucket, his wrecked-up but totally cool car.

I tried the back door, but it was locked. I rang the bell while I rummaged around in my backpack for my house keys. I could hear Shannon yipping like crazy in the kitchen.

When I let myself in, Shannon jumped all over me. I picked her up and called out, "Charlie, didn't you hear me?"

Then I spotted a handwritten note on the

kitchen table. I leaned over and read it:

Hi, Charlie and Kristy!
Picking up David Michael at
school — quite sick — will take
him to doctor — Emily Michelle
and Andrew with me — Karen
at art class — pray it doesn't
snow — Watson in Stamford
at a business meeting until
5:00 — help yourself to a snack.
Love,
Nannie
P.S. Charlie, don't forget to pick
up Sam at the A & P at
4:30 today.

Poor Nannie. Stuck in the snow with the Pink Clinker. That's the name of her car, which is old and pink and has over a hundred thousand miles on it.

Poor David Michael, too. I hoped he was okay.

I put Shannon down. On the table, next to the note, was an open bag of tortilla chips, two Yankee Doodle wrappers, and a plate with a half-eaten bagel and cream cheese.

Definite signs of Charlie.

"Charlie?" I called out.

Yap! Yap!

Shannon was not letting me alone. Obviously no one had taken her for a walk yet.

I knew where Charlie was. Hiding upstairs, trying to avoid dog-walking duty. Laughing at me. Grrrr.

"Creep!" I called out as loudly as I could. Then I said to Shannon, "Don't worry. *I* care about you."

I grabbed her leash from a hook in the mud room, fastened it to her collar, and opened the back door.

Shannon took off like a shot. I almost fell out the door. She led me around the house and onto McLelland, her tail wagging like crazy.

It was still pretty gray and chilly. "Let's make this a short one, huh?" I asked Shannon.

Guess again. Shannon wouldn't hear of it. When I tried to pull her back, she squealed as if I were trying to murder her.

Before long, we were in the wooded area beyond McLelland. Shannon loves to walk through there in the summertime to the tennis courts beyond, where she can sit and watch the players.

"Uh, Shannon, I hate to disappoint you," I said, "but the season hasn't — "

That was when I spotted the Junk Bucket in the parking lot beyond the court. (I guess the tire tracks I'd seen in the driveway had been made backing out of the garage, not going in.)

It was the only car there. I could see Charlie

inside — well, actually, the back of his head. He looked as if he were talking to someone.

As I walked closer, he turned slightly.

I stopped in my tracks. His face was . . . attached. To a girl's.

He wasn't talking. He was kissing!

I could feel my face turning red. Not that I was shocked or anything. I mean, kissing is no big deal. And Charlie *is* seventeen. He does have girlfriends.

But if he saw me, I was dead meat.

"Ssshhhhh," I said, picking up Shannon and backing away.

Now I knew what had happened. Charlie had arrived home with his latest girlfriend, Sarah. He expected Nannie, David Michael, Andrew, and Emily to be home, but the house was empty.

Mom has a strict rule about girlfriends. They are not allowed into the house if no adults are present. I know, it sounds like a dumb rule. And Charlie and Sam have both thrown fits about it. But Mom is stubborn, and my brothers know not to cross her.

So Charlie had obeyed. Sort of. He and Sarah had wolfed down a quick snack and left the house.

And then they'd gone parking.

Silently I walked back through the woods, and then onto the street. As I set Shannon down, I could not stop grinning.

"This is between you and me," I whispered.

But all I could think was, You'd better be nice to me, Charlie Thomas. I know your secret.

I jogged home behind Shannon. Clouds of snow puffed around my feet.

All of a sudden, the weather didn't seem so bad, after all.

CHAPTER 2

"Steeeeeee-ro-o-o-o-o-ike!" bellowed Bart Taylor. (Translation: "Strike!" in Bart's own baseball lingo.)

Linny Papadakis dropped his bat. "No way!" he protested. "You need an eye exam!"

"Hey, I do not . . . Ralph," Bart replied.

"Ralph?" Linny repeated.

Bart grinned. "Joke," he said. "Get it? Eye exam . . . Ralph?"

"Uh-huh," Linny said. (Or maybe it was "ha-ha." Whatever it was, I don't think he got it.) He scowled and lifted his bat to his shoulders. "Ball one."

"Come on, pitcher, straighten it out," I said, crouching behind the plate.

We were in my front yard, facing away from the house. Our "plate" was a trash can lid. It was still early March, weeks away from softball season. The snow had melted (yea!) but the air was still chilly. I was wearing a wool jacket, unbuttoned.

Most of the neighborhood kids were outside. My stepsister, Karen, was trying to teach my stepbrother, Andrew, how to ride a two-wheeler. Across the street, Melody Korman was playing catch with Timmy and Scott Hsu.

Bart and I were coaching an informal, off-season practice with some Krushers: Linny and his friend, Bill Korman, who are both nine; and my brother, David Michael, and Linny's sister, Hannie, who are seven. (In case you were worried, David Michael had had an ear infection but was fine now.)

Hannie, David Michael, and Bill were waiting impatiently in the "field." Linny waved his bat around, trying to look like a major leaguer. He held his hand up grandly to call a timeout. He stepped back and looked agitated. He spat.

"Eeeeeww, gross!" cried Hannie.

Linny glared at her. "You're wrecking my concentration!"

"You're wrecking Kristy's lawn!" Hannie replied.

"Play ball!" Bill insisted.

Thud. Linny hit the next pitch. The ball rolled across the lawn. Hannie put her glove down, but the ball bounced against her bare right hand. "Owwwww!" she cried out.

14

"Butterfingers," Linny said.

"It really hurts, Linny!" Hannie cried, her eyes welling up.

Bill raced after the ball. Linny was circling the yard in slow motion, like a home run on video replay. He held his fist up and nodded to the imaginary cheering crowd.

When Bill threw the ball to me, I handed it to Hannie and pushed her toward Linny.

She tagged him hard.

"Yerrrrrrrr out!" Bart shouted.

"Yea, Hannie!" Melody cried from across the street.

"Hey, no fair!" Linny protested. "This isn't a real game!"

"I'm next batter!" David Michael called out.

As David Michael picked up the bat, Linny stormed into the field. He ignored his sister's triumphant grin.

I tried to keep from laughing. I didn't want Linny to think I was teasing him. The poor kid was in a bad enough mood.

Bart, on the other hand, was in hysterics. Giggling like crazy. Honestly, I wanted to smack him.

For a cute guy, Bart can be a jerk. Sometimes. Usually he's fun to be with. He's a good ballplayer, athletic and graceful. He has the deepest brown eyes, thick brown hair, and the most adorable lopsided smile.

Bart and I were going steady, sort of. Not boyfriend-girlfriend-kissyface-make-me-puke, like Charlie and Sarah, but hanging-out-and-going-to-dances-and-parties. For example, before the practice that day, he'd asked me to go to a movie the next weekend and I had said, "Cool." That was about the tone of it. Pretty low key.

"Come on, Bart Man, pitch the ball," I said.

Bart lobbed an underhand pitch to David Michael. It was way too low.

Smmmmmack! I don't know how, but David Michael really whacked it.

It sailed over Linny, Hannie, and Bill, right into the street.

"Heads up!" Bart yelled.

"Home run! Home run!" David Michael shouted.

"Pop fly," Linny muttered. (What a sport.)

Hannie ran after the ball. Across the street, Melody and the Hsu boys were running after it, too.

Timmy reached it first. He reared back and threw. It sailed sideways, down the street. (Timmy, I feel obligated to say, is *not* a Krusher.)

Luckily Karen and Andrew were just rounding the corner. Karen fielded the ball and threw it back.

"I want to bat!" Andrew yelled, climbing off his bike.

"Me, too," Hannie said.

"I call first!" Scott shouted.

"Second!" Karen chimed in.

"Okay, alphabetically by first names!" I yelled.

"I change my name to Aaron!" Bill said.

"Alphabetically backward," Bart replied.

Bill grinned. "I'm Zack!"

The kids were all crowding around home plate. Bart was shaking his head, laughing like crazy. "What's so funny?" I asked.

"Typical Krushers," he replied.

"Oh? What's *that* supposed to mean?" I said.

"Nothing."

What a goon. See, Bart coaches the Bashers, the Krushers' number one (and only) rival. His team is bigger, older, and more organized than ours. But guess who won our World Series last season?

The Krushers, of course.

"Jealous," I mumbled.

Bart smirked. "We let you guys win, you know."

"Did not!" David Michael yelled.

"Crush the Bashers! Crush the Bashers!" Linny chanted.

The rest of the kids joined right in.

I smiled at Bart. "You're outnumbered."

I organized sides for a practice. Most of the kids were pretty rusty, but with my help, just about everyone was making contact with the ball. Even the non-Krushers, Timmy and Scott, were having a great time. At one point, Scott asked, "Can we join the team?"

"Well, I don't know," Bart spoke up. "Our tryouts aren't till the spring, and — "

"I don't want to join *your* team." Timmy rolled his eyes. "I meant the Krushers."

I smiled. "Sure, guys. No tryout necessary for the World Champs."

"Yeaaaaaa!" Scott and Timmy jumped up and down.

Bart tried not to look insulted.

"Can we have an official practice?" Bill asked. "Like, on the field, with uniforms and stuff?"

"Yeah!" Melody said. "It's almost spring."

Bart shook his head. "We're still in our down coats."

"Mine is Hollofil, not down," Karen informed us.

"The *pros* are already in spring training," Bill insisted.

"Yeah, in Florida," Bart replied.

"Can we go there?" Andrew asked.

"That is a plane ride away," Karen patiently told him.

Andrew lit up. "Okay!"

"Sorry, guys," I said. "We really need to wait a month or so."

"To fly?" Andrew asked.

"No, to begin official team practice," Bart said.

Melody sank to the ground, arms folded. "No fair."

"Look, guys, softball's a warm-weather game," I said firmly. "We're still in snow season. And we can't move around well with bulky clothes on. Plus the ground is rock-hard until the spring thaw. Besides, what's wrong with working on our basics right here?"

"We've had enough basics," David Michael complained.

"This isn't real," Linny said.

"I'm bored," Bill added.

"We could play Parcheesi," Karen suggested.

"How about a game of football?" Bart asked.

"Ewwww," said Hannie and Bill.

"Want to shoot baskets?" Bart pushed on.

David Michael shook his head. "The basketball has a hole. It's flat."

Chug . . . ding . . . dzzzzt. The famous Kristy Thomas Idea Machine was at work.

"Do you know what the world record for flatball free throws is?" I asked.

The kids looked at me as if I were speaking Turkish.

"Zilch," I continued. "Absolutely no one in the entire world has kept track of consecutive successful free throws with a flattened basketball, and that's a fact."

Linny burst out laughing. *"Flattened basketball? That's not an official statistic!"*

Bart shrugged. "We'll make it official."

"It has to be printed," Linny insisted. "Like the *Guinness Book of World Records.*"

"Fine," I said. "Then let's print it. In the *Official Thomas Book of World Records.*"

"Who's Thomas?" Melody asked.

"Kristy Thomas," I shot back. "You guys set the records, I'll record them."

Bart nodded enthusiastically. "The weirder the better."

"Fastest tree climber," Bill suggested.

"Most books read in one week," Karen offered.

"That's not weird," Linny remarked.

"How about, most holes in one shirt," David Michael piped up. (He was in a shirt-poking phase.)

"Most toe boogers!" Hannie squealed.

I could tell that was a keeper. The kids were rolling on the lawn, cackling.

"Uh, excuse me?" I asked.

"You know," Hannie said, "the stuff that's between your toes when you take your socks off at night?"

"Cool." Bart started to take his shoes off.

Of course, so did all the others. Despite the cold.

"Not now!" I yelled. "This is one you can do later, in private."

I shot Bart another Look. Grinning, he jumped to his feet. "Last one to the flatball has to collect the toe boogers!"

They were off like a cannon shot.

And I had a new project on my hands.

CHAPTER 3

"Aren't you going a *little* overboard?" Claudia asked.

"A little?" Abby said. "Toss her the life preservers."

"Kristy," Mallory calmly explained, "I don't think I can ask Henrietta Hayes to — "

"You were her assistant!" I reminded her. "She's one of the most famous authors around. She knows tons of publishers. Just call to say hi, how're you doing. Then you can casually say, 'I have this friend who has a great book idea.' "

"Kristyyyy," Stacey warned her.

Mallory was shaking her head firmly.

I tried Claudia. "You had Ted Garber on your radio show. Another world-class writer. You could call him."

"Yeah, right, Kristy. Teddy babe and I, we're like this." Claudia held up two fingers close together.

Okay, maybe I'm crazy. But think about it. When you go into a bookstore, you always see some new, weird humor book on display. So what could be newer and weirder than *Record Wreckers: The Thomas Book of Kids' Wild, Wacko, Off-the-Wall Records*? Wouldn't you want to buy it?

Well, I would.

Which was why I had brought the subject up at our Monday Baby-sitters Club meeting. Henrietta Hayes and Ted Garber are two of the hottest children's book authors in the country — two great BSC connections to the world of publishing! What was so terrible about asking them for a teeny tiny favor?

I know, I know. Some people just don't see the light, even if they trip over it.

Sigh.

I decided to let the subject brew for awhile. I'd bring it up later. We had a full half hour.

That's how long our meetings last, from five-thirty to six, every Monday, Wednesday, and Friday. That isn't a long time, and boy, do we fill it up.

Our number one activity: answering phone calls from Stoneybrook parents. Our clients love us. They call one number and reach seven great sitters. And we spread out the jobs evenly, so we all keep busy.

Fantastic idea, isn't it? (If I do say so myself.)

But, unfortunately, not perfect. I did have to work out some kinks. For instance, the diversity problem. Some clients didn't like the idea of seven different sitters, instead of one or two steady ones. So we try to be super prepared. We write about each of our jobs in the BSC notebook, including special house rules, bedtimes, and any other useful information about the client or the children. *Voilà* — each member is up-to-date for each client.

The notebook was my idea. (Ahem.) So were Kid-Kits. Those are small boxes full of old toys, games, and books that we sometimes take to our jobs. Kids love them.

As you can see, the BSC is well run. I should know. As I mentioned, I'm the president. I'm in charge of the meetings. I also try out different advertising techniques to find new clients. Kristy's Cardinal Rule of Business is *There's no such thing as too much business.*

Some of the other members think I'm crazy. Claudia, for instance. She's our vice-president, mainly because we use her room as our headquarters (she has her own private phone line). Claud's always teasing me, telling me to chill out.

I don't mind. I'm used to her. I lived across the street from Claudia almost my whole life. It's impossible to stay angry at her. For one thing, she has the best sense of humor. For another, she feeds us great junk food at our meetings. Chocolates, cookies, chips, pretzels. You name it, Claudia has it hidden away in every corner of her room.

Well hidden. Her parents would pass out if they knew she was such a junk food addict. They are super-strict about nutrition. (Education, too. Claudia has to hide her Nancy Drew books, because Mr. and Mrs. Kishi consider them unchallenging.)

Too much chocolate is supposed to make you fat, pimply, and irritable, right? Not Claud. She's thin, zitless, and fun-loving. Gorgeous, too. Her hair is jet-black and looks so cool, whether it's in braids, a ponytail, corn-rows, or even hanging loose. (When my hair hangs loose, I look like a wet mouse.)

Boy, is Claudia different from the brainy, conservative types who make up the rest of her family. Her older sister, Janine, for example, is a real certified genius. Claudia's a terrible student (especially in spelling and math), but she's an amazingly talented artist. Even the way she dresses is like an abstract painting — vintage clothes, funky odds and ends from thrift stores. I don't know how she does it, but she always looks great.

The Kishis used to compare Claudia to Janine all the time. But they've grown out of that, more or less. The one family member who always understood Claudia was her grand-mother, Mimi. Mimi's English wasn't perfect (Claud's grandparents immigrated to the United States from Japan), but she was Claudia's soulmate. Since she died, Claudia has kept a large picture of Mimi on her wall, and a smaller one on her night table, right next to the phone.

Rrrrring!

Our first call came in at 5:29.

Stacey picked up the receiver. "Baby-sitters Club," she said. "Hey, Mrs. Pike! Mallory's right here. . . . Sure, I'll tell her. . . . Okay, we'll get back to you."

As Stacey hung up, Claudia's clock flicked to 5:30. "This meeting will come to order!" I announced.

"Aye-aye, sir," said Claudia with a yawn. (Honestly, I get no respect.)

"Your mom and dad have an emergency PTO meeting Saturday and need you and one of us to sit," Stacey told Mallory. "Also, she wants you to borrow the toilet plunger from the Kishis'. Claire flushed some doll accessories."

Mal looked horrified. "I have to walk home with one of those things? In public?"

I tried not to laugh, but I couldn't help it. The image was too funny.

We all started howling like hyenas. Except

Mary Anne, who was politely looking through the BSC record book. "Abby, Stacey, and Kristy are free," she said.

"Uh, well," Stacey said, "Robert asked me to — "

Abby raised her hand. "I'll take the plunge."

The rest of us groaned.

As Mary Anne wrote Abby's name on the record book calendar, Stacey tapped out the Pikes' number.

The record book is the backbone of the BSC. Without it, we'd be lost. Along with the calendar of sitting jobs, it contains a list of client names, addresses, and pay rates. Mary Anne is in charge of it. As club secretary, she assigns our jobs. She has to know in advance every BSC member's conflicts: doctor appointments, afterschool activities, lessons, and practices. She also has to keep the list updated.

Confusing? Not to Mary Anne. Organized isn't the word for her. Even efficient doesn't come close. Organicient? Something like that. But that's just one side of her. She happens to be the warmest, sweetest, most sensitive person around. Shy, too.

And she's the best friend of yours truly. She and her dad lived next door to me in my old neighborhood. (I never knew Mrs. Spier. She died when Mary Anne was a baby.) Mr. Spier was very strict and never seemed to realize

Mary Anne was growing up. Even in seventh grade, she had to wear pigtails and little-girl dresses to school, and she wasn't allowed to get her ears pierced.

Mr. Spier may be stuffy, but he's not a monster. Gradually he began to ease up. And eventually, after so many years of single parenthood, he remarried — the divorced mom of another BSC member, Dawn Schafer! Dawn, her mom, and her brother had moved to Stoneybrook from California. But Mrs. Schafer had grown up here, and Mr. Spier was an old flame of hers from high school. What a soap opera, huh? Boy, did Mary Anne love having a stepsister in the house. Unfortunately, Dawn has moved back to her dad's house in California. (Her brother's there, too; he'd already moved awhile ago.)

Nowadays Mary Anne looks her age. She has short brown hair and dark brown eyes. Before she had her hair cut, people used to say we looked alike. Which was true, I guess. No one, however, has ever said our personalities are alike. Mary Anne hates sports, and she cries at the slightest thing.

Shy as she is, Mary Anne's one of the two BSC members with a steady (meaning, kissy-face serious) boyfriend. His name is Logan Bruno, and he's an associate member of the BSC. That means he fills in whenever he can, but he doesn't have to attend meetings.

Our treasurer is Stacey. She collects dues every Monday and keeps the cash in a manila envelope. We use the money to contribute to Claudia's phone bill, pay Charlie for gas money (he drives Abby and me to meetings), and keep our Kid-Kits stocked. Sometimes, if we have a surplus, we'll treat ourselves to pizza.

Stacey is our only diabetic-native-New-Yorker-math-whiz-fashion-plate-member. Okay, I'll clarify all that. She has diabetes, which means her body doesn't properly make this hormone called insulin. Insulin regulates the sugar in your blood, and without it you can go into a coma. So Stacey has to inject insulin every day, eat very regular meals, and avoid sweets. (She eats chips and pretzels at our meetings.)

All of us occasionally have taken the train ride to New York with Stacey. Her dad still lives in an apartment there, and she visits him pretty often. I don't know about you, but I think NYC is the coolest place. (Although I haven't been able to convince Stacey to ask her dad to take us to Shea Stadium.) Stace is an only child. When she first moved to Stoneybrook, her parents were married but not getting along too great. Then they all had to move back to New York because of Mr. McGill's job, and the marriage fell apart. Stacey had to choose between living in the Big Apple with her dad or moving to Stoneybrook with her mom.

Why did she choose Stoneybrook? Her unbelievably fantastic friends, of course! But she still retains a little New Yorkishness. Mostly in the way she dresses: cool, urban, sophisticated. She wears stuff I would never dream of wearing. (Stacey calls me fashion-challenged.) She has long, blonde hair, and is the only other member with a steady boyfriend. *Very* steady. Not long ago, Stacey became so involved with him, she started missing meetings and backing out of jobs. I was so furious at her, I kicked her out of the BSC.

(Don't worry, we made up.)

Our alternate officer is Abby Stevenson, whom you already know about. She's the official substitute whenever another officer is absent.

Jessica (Jessi) Ramsey and Mallory Pike are our two junior officers. They're in sixth grade (the rest of us are in eighth). They both have early curfews on school nights, so they take a lot of weekend and afternoon jobs.

Jessi is a future ballet star, mark my words. Even I enjoy watching her, and normally I'd rather eat leftover turnips than go to a ballet.

Her other great passion is horses. I think she and Mallory have watched both *Black Beauty* videos about a hundred times.

The Ramseys moved here from New Jersey. They're African-American, and you would not believe the bigotry they faced in Stoneybrook. Really, it came from just a few creeps, but it was enough to make things uncomfortable for them. Fortunately, the people involved seem to have come to their senses since then.

Mal is Jessi's best friend. They both moan about how hard it is being the oldest child in the family. Jessi has two younger siblings, a sister and a brother, and Mal has seven. Yup, seven. That's why her parents often need two sitters. A traffic cop would be nice, too. The Pike house is twenty-four-hour chaos. It makes our house look peaceful. I keep telling Mal she could have a family softball team, but she hates sports. Her favorite activities are writing and illustrating her own stories.

Those are our regular members. You already know about one of our associate members, Logan Bruno. The other is Shannon Kilbourne. She goes to a private school called Stoney-brook Day (so does Bart). She couldn't possibly be a regular member because she's so involved in extracurricular activities. Some-how, though, Shannon always manages to come through in a clutch. She pinch-hit for us a lot after Dawn moved and before Abby joined.

Okay, now I've told you about the rules, the players, and the positions.

Back to the game.

Until about 5:50, we continued to take more calls. Then, finally, I brought up *Record Wreckers* again.

"No!" was the first word out of Claudia's mouth. "I will not call Ted Garber!"

"Forget about Ted Garber," I said. "Let's just talk about the book itself. What do you think?"

"The idea is fantastic," Claudia replied. "If you just keep it simple."

"Without worrying about fame and fortune," Stacey added.

"My brothers and sisters would die to be in it," Mallory said.

"That's what I'm talking about!" I blurted out. "Get as many kids involved as we can. Turn it into a BSC project."

Mary Anne's brows were all scrunched up. "But what about the little kids, the ones who aren't as good in sports?"

"It doesn't have to be sports," I answered. "Kids can make up records. You know . . . consecutive times saying the word 'rutabaga' without stopping. The number of cornflakes balanced on one nose."

Jessi raised an eyebrow. "Cornflakes on your nose?"

"Whatever!" I said. "The stupider the better. The littlest kids can be involved. We'll do it for a month or so, then collect the results. It'll be so much fun!"

Falling off their seats. Screaming with laughter. That's how I expected my friends to react.

Instead, they all looked as if they were concentrating on a final exam. Just glancing at each other, thinking.

They hated it. Thought it was the stinkiest idea since extended-wear socks. Couldn't bear to tell me the truth.

"Well?" I said.

Claudia smiled. "I don't know, guys," she said. "Maybe we *should* try to get it published."

"Can't you just see it on the book club order form?" Mallory said.

Everybody started talking at once, thinking of ideas for dumb world records.

Bingo.

Hey, I told you my friends were cool.

CHAPTER 4

Some people are huge movie fans. Not me. I can think of a million better places to be than a dark, crowded room for two hours on a sunny day.

Sometimes, however, I make an exception. That Saturday morning, for instance. I was excited about going to the Stoneybrook Cinema. First of all, I was going with Bart. Second, the movie was a thriller called *Missing Pieces*, which Stacey and Robert had seen and loved.

I biked over to Bart's around eleven o'clock. (I *hate* being late.) He was standing on his porch with a couple of other guys.

"Hi!" I called out, wheeling my bike up the walkway.

"Heyyyy!" Bart replied with a big grin.

The two other boys looked at me for a moment, then shot each other a glance.

"These are my friends from Stoneybrook Day, Kevin and Seth," Bart said. "They were just leaving. Guys, this is Kristy, my girl-friend."

Huh?

Girlfriend?

He said that so casually, I almost didn't notice. It was as if he were saying "my teammate" or something.

I nodded. "Hi."

The guys muttered hellos and nice-to-meet-yous.

As they left, I could see Kevin throwing Bart a thumbs-up sign. As if to say, *Nice work.*

Real mature.

I thought of saying something, but I didn't. I mean, calling me a girlfriend isn't a total lie, really. It just sounds a little funny.

Oh, well. Maybe Bart was carried away with his feelings when he saw me. Can you blame him? (Harrrrumph.)

If the other guys wanted to be jerks, that was their problem.

"Ready to go?" I asked.

Bart checked his watch. "Now? We have almost an hour."

"What if it sells out?"

Shaking his head, Bart went back into his house. I could hear him telling his parents he was leaving.

Moments later we were biking toward downtown Stoneybrook. But first we had to pass the local ballfields. "Last one to the other side buys the popcorn!" I said.

I tore away, down the bike path that circles behind the outfield. Bart tried to cut across. He would have won easily, but the ground was so hard and rutted, he nearly fell off. (I *knew* that would happen.)

I waited for him at the other side, buffing my nails.

"No fair!" he shouted as he approached.

"No butter, lots of salt, please," I replied.

Bart grumbled the rest of the way.

When we arrived at Stoneybrook Cinema, the ticket seller wasn't even there yet. So Bart and I bought a couple of candy bars at a store and sat on one of the benches along Main Street. Bart put his arm behind me, across the top of the bench.

"Everyone's psyched about *Record Wreckers*," I said. "Abby and Mallory are going to tell the Pike kids about it when they sit today."

"Without you?" Bart asked.

"Sure. Why not? The whole BSC is involved."

"I know. But it was your idea."

"You helped me think of it, you know."

"Great minds think alike."

I smiled. Bart's hand landed on my shoulder and he pulled me toward him. He was being so sweet.

An older couple passed us and nodded a greeting. I felt a little embarrassed. As I watched, they bought tickets for the movie.

"Come on, it's open," I said. "Let's find good seats."

Bart bought the popcorn — no butter, lots of salt — and two sodas, and we walked into the theater. Bart began edging into the third-to-the-back row.

"Too far," I said. "Let's go closer."

Bart was already plopping himself into a seat. "I bought the popcorn," he said with a grin, "so I get to choose where we sit."

"Maybe we can rent binoculars," I remarked.

But I sat. As the lights dimmed, I reached for the popcorn.

Bart put his arm around the back of my seat. "Is it salty enough?" he asked.

"Fome," I replied. (I was trying to say *fine*, but my mouth was full.)

Bart's arm landed on my shoulder as the previews came on.

The movie's opening scene was so exciting, I forgot about my appetite. It quickly spun into a complicated plot about an international smuggling ring. A car chase, a disappearing motorboat, a footrace over some city rooftops — I loved it.

Eventually the movie bogged down in the

love scene, when the male and female leads do just what everyone has expected them to do.

I could feel my eyelids growing heavier. On-screen, an actor playing a spy was looking all gooey-eyed at an undercover policewoman. His big face looked closer . . . closer . . . so close you could see his skin pores . . .

I felt something warm on my left cheek.

I jerked back. Bart was inches away, leaning over my seat.

He laughed. I laughed. I settled into my seat.

And then Bart kissed me.

Full on the lips. Right there in the back of the dark movie theater.

How did it feel? Well, it's not as if Bart and I had never kissed before. We had. We're not babies. Kissing is no big thing. I didn't yell or say "yuck" or try to spit out his germs.

I returned the kiss, just a short one, and we turned back to watch the movie.

It felt fine.

Now Bart's arm was around my shoulder. Which was kind of nice.

At first.

The problem was, he kept it there forever. My neck muscles started to ache. My shoulders began to sweat. I finally shifted around, trying to send a hint. Bart lifted his arm to give me some room. Then, *plop*, down it went.

About halfway through the movie, I reached around and lifted it off. Gently. With a smile.

Bart smiled back. As our arms came down toward the armrest, Bart held my hand.

And then he pulled me close and kissed me again.

Okay, no big deal. No one was sitting behind us, and the movie was in another dull spot.

But the third time Bart leaned over, the killer was running from a huge manhunt.

I couldn't look away. My face was turned to the left, kissing Bart, but my eyes were straining to the right.

How could Bart not be watching this? I glanced back at him, but I noticed his eyes were closed.

Boy, did that make me feel weird. As if I were spying on him. As if I should close *my* eyes, just to be fair.

As if I were responsible for his missing the show.

Was I supposed to close my eyes? Why? Just because people in the movies kiss that way? But they're supposed to be passionately in love. They're movie actors, not Kristy and Bart.

Besides, Bart was pressing too hard. Jamming my lips against my teeth.

I tried to say "Bart," but it came out more like "Bloob."

He opened his eyes. "Huh?"

"Uh, this is the good part," I replied, glancing at the screen.

"Oh."

We watched. But now I wasn't thinking about the movie. I felt kind of like a fool. Had I done something wrong? Had I been rude? Had I hurt Bart's feelings?

Whatever. For the rest of the movie, Bart stayed in his seat and I could concentrate again. By the end, we were both practically jumping and cheering.

Have you ever seen a movie so complicated you couldn't stop talking about it after you left? This one was like that.

As we went out to where our bikes were locked, our mouths were going a mile a minute. We didn't stop even when we were riding.

We decided to continue our conversation at Pizza Express.

As usual on a Saturday afternoon, the place was crowded. But Bart and I managed to find a booth in the back. We ordered two sodas and a pizza with anchovies. (I know, it's weird, but we both like them.)

When the waiter left, Bart began fiddling with his water glass. "That was fun," he said.

"Yup," I replied.

"I'm glad we like the same kind of movie."

"Uh-huh."

Bart took a long sip. I took one from my glass, too. He began fidgeting and looking uncomfortable.

The kissing. That was what he wanted to talk about, I knew. Which was fine. I kind of wanted to, also. But I didn't want to be the one to bring it up. What would I say? *Uh, excuse me, Bart, but could we keep the kissing to a minimum, and not during the exciting parts?*

Finally Bart said, "So, um, I guess we can, like, go to the April Fools' Day dance at my school, right?"

"Are you asking me?" I asked.

"Well, yeah. I am. Don't you want to go?"

"Sure, we can go. Great."

"You want to?"

"Yes. That's what I said."

Bart was beaming. "All riiight."

Was that what this was all about? Was that why Bart was acting like this? Because of a dance?

Boys are so goony.

CHAPTER 5

Saturday

Today was Day One of Record Wreckers.
Ha. You mean Sitter
Breakers. (Oops. Did
I say that?)

Oh, come on, Abby. It was fun.
I know. I know. I'm
just being grumpy.
I don't mind losing
half my hair, Mal.
Baldness is so cool.

You're not bald! Now, come on, let's write
about our job.
Right. Let's see. It
was a dark and
stormy night....

It was not a dark and stormy night. That's just Abby's warped sense of humor. Actually, it was the same bright, sunny afternoon on which Bart and I had gone to the movies.

Oh, and don't worry about Abby's hair. It didn't look too bad. Considering what had happened.

Let me start from the beginning.

Abby arrived at the Pike house prepared for the worst. She wore old clothes and pulled her hair into a ponytail. And she had borrowed my metal whistle.

Sitting for Mal's younger siblings is not for the faint-hearted. You have to be part traffic cop, part referee, and part camp counselor. If you survive a job with them, you can sit for anyone.

No, they're not awful kids. Just numerous. Seven, to be exact. The oldest are ten-year-old triplets named Adam, Jordan, and Byron. (Sometimes one of them volunteers to be the second sitter. But mostly, they can't be bothered.) Next is Vanessa, who's nine; Nicky, eight; Margo, seven; and Claire, five.

As Abby went up the Pikes' front walk, the house was shaking. Well, that's what she claims. She heard wild whooping and laughing inside. She gathered her inner strength and pressed the doorbell.

"Aaaaabbyyyyyyy!" a happy cry rang out.

The door flew open. There stood the entire clan, spilling over with joyful energy. An image of the Brady Bunch popped into Abby's mind.

"Can we start?" Adam asked.

"Start what?" Abby asked back.

"The records!" Margo and Nicky shouted.

"You put on any records," Mr. Pike's voice rang out, "and you have to put them back."

"Not *those* kinds of records, Daddy-silly-billy-goo-goo," Claire said.

The others broke out laughing, chattering, bragging, challenging each other, and predicting victory.

Mr. and Mrs. Pike walked into the living room, looking totally confused. Quickly they gave Abby and Mal some last-minute instructions and hurried out.

"Okay, let's go over the rules," Mallory said.

"Rule number one," Abby announced. "You must have fun." (Good old Abby.)

"YEEAAAAAAA!"

"Rule number two," Mallory said. "Your record must be set in the presence of a BSC member."

"And we have to approve the event," Abby added. "No stuff like 'Most times beating up a younger brother.'"

"Rats," Adam murmured.

"How about a younger sister?" Nicky asked.

Claire whapped him with a rag doll.

"Okay, guys," Abby said. "On your mark, get set, go!"

Utter, complete pandemonium.

(Honestly, I don't know how the Pikes' neighbors can stand it. They all must have earplugs.)

Like a herd of wild yak, the kids tramped through the house. Mal ran to her room to get a notebook.

Abby went into the kitchen, where Byron and Jordan were rummaging around in the cupboards.

Margo emerged from the coat closet with her arms full of caps and hats, dropped them on the kitchen table, then plunged into the closet again.

As Mal came downstairs, holding a spiral notebook, Jordan and Byron set an open box of Cap'n Crunch between them on the kitchen counter.

"Most Crunch catches, by mouth," Byron announced.

He tossed a nugget of cereal into the air and leaned his head back, mouth wide open. The cereal bonked him on the chin and bounced onto the floor.

Next Jordan gave it a try, and he caught one. "One," he said.

Margo raced in with another load of hats. "Okay, here I go. Help me keep count."

She put her dad's huge fur hat on and said, "One."

From the den, Nicky called out, "Somebody come in here!"

"I'll go," Abby volunteered.

Mal gave her some sheets from the notebook. Abby rushed into the den.

There, she found Nicky sitting on a sofa, watching a cartoon.

"Uh, hello?" Abby said. "Did we forget about our records?"

Nicky checked his watch. "One minute, fourteen seconds."

"Of what?" Abby asked.

"TV watching."

"Ehhhhhh!" Abby made a noise like a game show buzzer. "Wrong. Not approved."

Nicky stomped away. Then Adam burst in with Vanessa, who was holding a big math textbook and a pencil.

"Speed multiplication, the fastest in the nation," Vanessa the Obsessive Rhymer announced, as she and Adam plopped down on opposite sides of the couch. Opening up the book, she said, "Abby, you time Adam."

Abby looked at her watch. "Okay . . . go."

"Five times six," Vanessa snapped.

"Thirty," Adam shot back.

"Nine times eight!"

Claire ran in, all excited. She was holding the Pikes' basset hound, Pow. "I know! Most times hopping on one foot with a doggie!" she cried. "One, two, three, four, five . . ."

"Clai-*aire*! You're interrupting!" Adam yelled. "I call a do-over!"

" . . . Nine, ten, eleven . . ." Claire was already starting to poop out. She can barely hold Pow. And poor Pow was not enjoying all the jouncing.

Not to mention poor Abby.

"Ahhh-CHOOOOOO!" she sneezed. "Uh, Claire, would you bide lettig Pow idto the backyard? I'b allergic."

Claire's feet hit the ground. "But what about my record?"

"You set it!" Abby quickly declared. "No wud id the world has ever jubped elevid tibes holdig a dog! Codgratulashuds!"

"Yippee!" Claire ran to the back door, planting kisses all over Pow.

"Ah — ahhh — " Abby dashed into the kitchen.

Mallory was already looking for the tissues.

"They're over there!" Margo said.

As she pointed, the hats fell from her head

onto the floor. They landed in a pile of Cap'n Crunch.

"Oh, n-o-o-o-o!" cried Margo.

"You broke my concentration!" yelled Jordan.

"Nine!" announced Byron.

"*CHOOOO!*" sneezed Abby.

"Stop!" Claire's voice screamed from outside. "Nicky's hitting me with Twinkies!"

Abby blew her nose. Margo began loading hats again. Jordan started flipping Cap'n Crunches. Byron sat down and moaned from a cereal overload. Vanessa and Adam began speed multiplying in the den again.

Mal ran out the back door, just in time to see a plastic-wrapped missile hurtle across the yard.

"Roo-o-o-o!" yowled Pow, running after it.

"No, Pow, stay!" Nicky shouted.

Too late. The moment the Twinkie landed, Pow was on it.

"Ohhhh, that was the farthest one!" Nicky said.

That was when Mal noticed the other Twinkies — one near the garage, another in a barren rosebush. And one at the feet of Claire, who was standing in the middle of the yard.

"Can I try one?" Claire pleaded.

Mallory put Pow back into the doghouse. She was about to tell Claire and Nicky to stop wasting the Twinkies, but she didn't.

Claire wasn't angry anymore. She and Nicky were dividing up the remaining missiles, giggling like crazy.

With a sigh, Mallory wrote TWINKIE TOSS at the top of a sheet of paper.

Abby stayed with the indoor events. She timed Vanessa and Adam (Vanessa won), then recorded Margo's hat record (nine) and Byron and Jordan's contest (Byron had twelve consecutive catches).

Afterward, they all went outside. Margo joined the Twinkie toss. Claire and Vanessa were off cooking up another idea.

The triplets disappeared into the garage. A moment later they emerged with their bikes and an air pump with a pressure gauge. Immediately they began letting the air out of their tires.

"Fastest tire pumper," Byron explained. "Full is forty pounds."

Abby knelt down, looking at her watch. "Say when."

That was when she felt the splat on the back of her head.

"Oops," Claire's voice meekly rang out.

For a moment the yard fell silent.

Abby didn't like the sound of that. She reached around and felt something warm and sticky in her hair.

"Claire, what did you do?" Mallory snapped.

"It was Vanessa!" Claire yelled back.

Vanessa was turning red. "I didn't think it would go so far."

"It was a bubblegum spit," Claire explained.

Abby stood up. She tried to pull the wad out. But it was the soft and gooey kind. When she lifted her fingers away, they were stuck to long strands of gum and matted hair.

"Eeeewwwww!" Margo squealed.

"Oh, no!" Abby moaned. She ran inside and brought out a jar of peanut butter. Rubbing it into gummed hair is supposed to work. Well, it didn't. She tried ice cubes, another cure.

Oh for two.

As a last resort, Mallory ran inside to find the scissors. The others just stood there, gawking.

And Abby — strong, cheerful Abby — began to cry.

Oh, well.

No one ever said this job would be easy.

CHAPTER 6

"Grounder," Bart called.

Thwack! He hit a sharp ground ball to my left. Way to my left. I lunged for it and did a bellyflop onto the field.

The ball bounced past me.

"Whoa, what a try!" Bart yelled. "The official scorer calls it a hit!"

In case you don't know, that was supposed to be a compliment. By saying it was a hit, Bart was also saying it wasn't an error. In other words, it wasn't my fault the ball went past me. (Okay, you sports-challenged types, you can wake up now.)

It was Tuesday, after school. The sun was out, and the air was warm enough for me to wear just a down vest and sweater. Bart and I were on one of the ballfields, fine-tuning our skills.

I chased after the ball and threw it back. "Aim it, batter," I said.

"Pop fly," Bart replied.

This time he hit the ball much more accurately. Unfortunately, the sun was setting just behind the path of the ball.

The ball plopped to the ground behind me.

"Now you're looking like a Krusher!" Bart exclaimed.

That was *not* a compliment.

"You're asking for it, Taylor!" I said.

Bart grinned. "Oh, yeah? Asking for what?"

"Another horrible, humiliating defeat in the World Series."

"Ha! We were just being nice. Next time we won't give it to you."

That did it. I ran for him. Bart dropped his bat and sprinted away. "Come on, show that blazing Krusher speed!"

Hooting and laughing, he zigzagged across the field. I managed to corner him by the backstop and I wrestled him to the ground.

"Stop! Truce!" he pleaded, still laughing.

"Take it back," I commanded.

"What, the truth?" Bart replied.

I unleashed my ultimate weapon. I dug my fingers into his armpits. "Take it back!"

"Hoooo ha ha ha!" (Bart is very ticklish.) "Okay, okay, I take it back!"

I stopped the torture. We both sat up, still out of breath from the chase.

Bart looked down at me with a big, warm

smile. He reached over and stroked my hair.

I think he wanted to kiss me again. But my hair was kind of sweaty and his fingers yanked against a knot.

"Yeeow!" I said.

Bart quickly took his hand away. His face was turning red. "Sorry."

I tried my best to smile. "Trying to put me on the disabled list, huh? Just like a Basher — you can't win fair and square."

"Ooooh, that was low, Kristy." Bart leaped to his feet. "Hit me a couple. I'll show you how a pro fields the ball."

(A pro? That's what I like about Bart. His modesty.)

We played a little while longer, until it started becoming dark. Then we walked back toward our neighborhood together. Bart carried the bat in his right hand. He put his left arm around me. For some reason, I noticed his fingers dangling off my shoulders, like a bunch of mini-bananas. I wanted to make a joke about them, but that would have been too rude.

"Want to do something Friday night?" he asked. "You know, pizza or a movie?"

"I can't," I said. "I have to baby-sit at home."

"Auughh, another sitting job!" Bart laughed. "My parents should book you at my house. Then I'd see you more often."

"Very funny," I said. "You could join the BSC, you know."

"I'm a guy."

"So? Logan's a member," I reminded him.

"Yeah, but that's because his girlfriend's in it," Bart said.

"He also happens to like baby-sitting," I replied. "Plus he's very good at it. Anyway, how about Friday after school?"

"Huh?"

"After school and before the BSC meeting. I'm supposed to go with Mary Anne and Logan to the Argo for a snack. Want to meet us there?"

"Sure."

Bart walked me to my house. We said a cheerful good-bye, and I stayed in a pretty good mood for awhile. I made a salad and chopped up ingredients for Watson's home-made tacos. But as I was setting the table, I started thinking about what Bart had said.

That's because his girlfriend's in it. That was how Bart saw Logan's BSC membership.

The remark bothered me, but I couldn't figure out why. I mean, it's sort of true. And Logan's free to have whatever reason he wants.

But Logan wasn't the point. Bart was. Why had he said that? To explain why *he* wasn't joining the BSC. Why he and Logan were different.

Logan, after all, had a girlfriend.

So what did that make me? A buddy? An acquaintance? What were all those kisses in the movie theater about?

Why was Bart sending me mixed signals?

Chill, Kristy, I told myself. It wasn't a big deal. I mean, Mary Anne and Logan were in deep LUV. Bart and I were in advanced LIKE.

When you thought about it, Bart was just telling the truth.

Still, the statement bugged me.

After school that Friday, Mary Anne, Logan, and I walked to downtown Stoneybrook. We chatted the whole way.

I don't know what we talked about. For some reason, I can only remember my hands. I couldn't figure out what to do with them.

Mary Anne was talking with hers, gesturing and making graceful shapes. Whenever she finished, I noticed Logan would immediately hold her hand. Not grab it. Not plop his arm on her shoulder and let his fingers dangle.

It looked so natural. Neither of them seemed even to think about it. As if they were made to walk hand-in-hand.

They looked so happy and comfortable.

I shoved my hands in my pockets and kept

them there the rest of the way to the diner.

The Argo has old-fashioned booths with carefully taped-up vinyl seats and old, yellowing travel photos on the walls. It's kind of funky, but the food is great.

As we were looking at the menu, Bart approached the table. "You would, perhaps, enjoy the baked lizard snot omelette?" he asked in a weird accent. "Or may I interest you in motor oil coffee?"

Logan laughed. The people at the table next to us looked as if they were about to lose their lunch.

As Bart sat next to me, he kissed me on the cheek.

"Awwww," Logan said with a sly grin.

"Lo-*gan!*" Mary Anne nudged him in the ribs.

I don't know who was blushing more, Bart or Mary Anne.

Puh-leeze.

Keeping my dignity, I scanned the menu.

"May I help you?" asked a waiter.

I wasn't very hungry, for some reason. "Just a green salad," I answered. "With some crackers. And a club soda."

Bart made a face. "Bird food. Uh, I'll have a cheeseburger, fries, and cream soda."

When the waiter looked away, I crossed my eyes at Bart.

Across the table, Mary Anne and Logan were sharing a menu, busily discussing what to order.

"We'd like to share the taco salad," Logan finally said, "no olives, please."

"And a side order of fries," Mary Anne added, "a Diet Slice and a root beer."

"Thanks for ordering the fries," Logan said as the waiter left. "I forgot."

Mary Anne smiled. "I knew you'd want them. And the root beer."

"Awww," Bart teased.

Logan pretended to throw a roll at him. Then he said, "Kristy, you really started something with this world-record stuff. Last night, my brother and sister made a total mess of the kitchen trying to throw popcorn in the air and catch it."

"Mallory's brothers did that, too, with cereal," I said.

"Does that count as the same record?" Bart asked.

I thought about it a moment. "Well, they are two different materials."

"Maybe you can bring them together," Logan suggested. "Like a face-off."

"They can team up," Bart said. "You know, one person throws the stuff into the team-mate's mouth."

"I don't know . . ." I said.

"If a lot of kids are joining in, it would be fun for them to show their events to each other," Mary Anne said.

"Or demonstrate them to the public," I suggested. "After the book is done. By that time the weather will be nicer. We can charge admission. Maybe offer some baby-sitting hours as a door prize."

"And a trip to Las Vegas in your new minivan!" Logan blasted, in a TV announcer's voice.

Everyone laughed. I kicked Logan under the table.

"If the weather's nice, we can have it in my yard," Mary Anne reassured me. "On a day Logan doesn't have track practice."

We talked about plans until it was time for the meeting. Afterward, Bart walked with us part of the way, then veered off to go home.

Logan decided to attend the meeting. I tagged along behind him and Mary Anne.

I couldn't help but notice how comfortable they seemed. At the Argo, it was as if they could read each other's minds. They knew each other's schedules. They worked together.

Bart and I were not like that at all.

I had this funny feeling all the way to Claud's. I wasn't sure what it was, but it felt familiar.

It felt like jealousy.

CHAPTER 7

"I know an old lady who swallowed a crocodile . . ." sang Andrew in his bedroom.

"With a great big smile, she swallowed the crocodile . . ." answered David Michael from his bedroom.

From *her* room, Karen chimed in, "She swallowed the crocodile to catch the yak, she swallowed the yak to catch the platypus — "

"No!" Andrew shouted. "Gnu!"

"No gnus is good news!" David Michael called out.

They all howled at David Michael's joke. I could hear even little Emily Michelle giggling.

I glanced at my watch. Eight thirty-five. I had given them "lights-out" twenty minutes earlier. I was in the kitchen, trying to raid the fridge.

Instead, I trudged up the stairs. "Guys," I called out. "No more talking, please."

"But we have to set the record!" Karen protested.

The record, in case you haven't guessed, was the world's longest version of "I Know an Old Lady Who Swallowed a Fly."

"Continue tomorrow at breakfast," I said.

"But we won't remember what we thought up!" David Michael complained.

"You should have written it down," I replied.

"How could we? It's lights-out," Karen reminded me.

Touché. I retrieved my *Record Wreckers* book from my bedroom. I patiently wrote down about a hundred animals they'd managed to shove down that poor old lady's throat. Then I firmly said good night.

Record Fever had set in at the Brewer house, big-time. It had begun the moment I returned home from the day's BSC meeting. Here were some highlights:

Karen and David Michael tossed and caught an egg thirty-one times without dropping it. When it finally fell on the floor, we discovered for the first time that the egg was not hard-boiled.

Andrew set a spaghetti-sucking record (twenty-seven strands). For about a half hour afterward, his jaw was so sore he could barely talk.

Even Emily entered the book. She stroked Shannon fifty-three times with a brush before losing interest.

And those were just the records set before dinner. Which I had to serve, alone. Mom and Watson were at a dinner party, Sam and Charlie were at a high-school basketball game, and Nannie was playing in a bowling tournament.

After dinner I watched the building of the World's Highest Lego Tower and judged the World's Most Realistic Fake Sneeze. Those were fun. But soon the records degenerated.

Most Soap Bubbles Blown into an Open Toilet, Longest Burp, Most Grapes in a Mouth, the Best Mirror Toothpaste Mural . . .

When I saw Andrew and David Michael flinging boogers, I knew it was bedtime.

" . . . Her hair was curled, 'cause she swallowed the world . . ." Karen's voice wafted down from the second floor.

"HARRRRRRRUMPH!" I bellowed.

Giggles, then silence.

I was totally exhausted. And you know what? I had to do the same thing the next day. I had planned a record-setting tournament in our yard, with all the neighborhood kids. Abby had agreed to help.

It was going to be a long weekend.

I took a box of pretzels from the kitchen, went into the den, and turned on the TV. I was in luck. A Mets spring-training exhibition game had just begun.

I threw myself on the sofa.

"Ahhhhh . . ." I murmured. Peace at last. Some down time for good old me.

With two outs in the bottom of the first, the doorbell rang.

That was strange. It was only 8:55. Mom and Watson weren't supposed to be home until eleven. Sam and Charlie's game was probably at halftime. And Nannie always goes out with her friends after bowling.

Besides, none of them ever rang the bell. They all had keys.

Ding-dong!

I ran into the living room and looked out the bay windows.

Bart was standing at the front door. He saw me and waved.

I went to the door and opened it. "Hi! What are you doing here?"

Bart shrugged. "I was bored. Dad and Mom want to watch some dumb history show. I figured I'd come over and watch the game."

"Oh. Okay. It's on."

Don't get me wrong. I was happy to see him. But I would have been happier if I'd known he was going to visit. I had adjusted very nicely to being alone for awhile.

"I know, I know, I should have called," Bart

said, walking toward the kitchen, "but you said you had to sit for all the kids tonight, and I figured you were busy putting them to bed. So I didn't want to disturb you."

"It's okay," I replied.

In the kitchen, he opened the refrigerator and took out a bottle of cola. "You're mad."

"No, Bart, I'm not!"

"Because I just like to be with you, that's all. It's my favorite thing to do, you know."

Leave it to Bart. One minute you want to strangle him, the next you want to hug him.

I couldn't help but smile. "Come on, the Mets are down, one to nothing."

I took two glasses and followed him into the den. We sank into the sofa, munching pretzels and drinking soda.

In the top of the second, the Mets rallied. We cheered and high-fived a lot.

By the commercial, Bart had shrunk. At least it looked that way. He was sitting in the middle of the sofa, right in the crack between the two seat cushions. His arm was around the back of the couch, behind me. Which seemed really awkward.

"Aren't you uncomfortable?" I asked.

"A little, I guess." He slid out of the crack. Closer to me.

Now we were both sharing my little sofa cushion. "That's better," Bart said.

I took a sip from my soda glass. Bart slipped his arm off the sofa and around my shoulder.

When I put the glass down, Bart's face was about an inch from mine.

I glanced at the TV. Another commercial was blasting away. Bart's eyes were starting to close.

I closed mine, too. We kissed, to the music of Weed Wipeout lawn care products.

Bart kind of cradled my face with his hands. That felt nice. And he wasn't bruising my face, the way he did at the movie. His lips were cool and sweet from the soda. But I was beginning to run out of breath, so I pulled away.

We both laughed a little, gulping for air.

Now a car commercial was on. Bo-ring.

Kissing was much more fun. We started again. I hugged Bart, which turned my upper body toward his, so my neck didn't feel so strained. My back, however, felt all twisted. I swung my legs underneath me so I could turn all the way to the right.

"Oh! Uh . . . hmph."

A voice. By the door.

Not mine. Not Bart's.

Watson! my brain screamed.

I snapped backward, away from Bart.

Watson was standing in the doorway. Glaring. With an expression I'd never seen before.

As if he had just stumbled onto a murder scene, with the killer still there.

I was mortified. I felt as if a dam in my neck had opened and blood was rushing upward to my face. I could barely breathe.

"Hi."

Ugh. The word sounded so weak and stupid. More like a mouse squeak. I wanted to swallow it right back down.

Why hadn't I heard the front door open? Or the footsteps across the living room carpet?

"IN THE BOTTOM OF THE SECOND, THE LEFT FIELDER LEADS OFF . . ."

Drowned out by the TV. That was it. Of course. I should have turned the volume down.

Should have turned the volume down? I couldn't believe I had thought that. As if I had planned this. As if this kissing was such a terrible, dark secret.

"Whuck — " My throat choked off the word, so I cleared it. "What are you doing here?"

"Funny, I was going to ask the same question," Watson replied, "of Bart."

"Well, uh, we were watching the game and," Bart stammered, "um, you know — "

My mom appeared behind Watson. She had a big, friendly smile on her face. I felt as if a warm spring breeze had suddenly blown into the room.

The breeze lasted about a nanosecond. When she saw Bart her face fell, and I was back in the Siberian tundra again.

"Kristy, I — I'm not sure I believe what I'm seeing," Watson said. "You know we have a house rule about this."

I groped for words. "But — but — "

"I have said this time and again to your brothers, Kristin Amanda," my mom said, "and they've been very good about it. I never expected *you'd* be the one to — "

She cut herself off, taking a deep breath. "Watson, why don't you drive Bart home? Kristy and I have a great deal to talk about."

"Okay," Bart said sheepishly. He slunk out of the den behind Watson without saying good-bye.

Me? I felt as if I'd just been kicked in the stomach by a Tyrannosaurus rex.

The Charlie and Sam rule. That's what she was talking about! The no-girlfriends-in-the-house-without-parents-present rule.

I had never thought about it. Never thought it could possibly have anything to do with me.

How stupid I was. Of course it did. If it applied to girlfriends, it applied to boyfriends, too. And no matter how I thought of Bart, *boyfriend* was the definition that fit this situation.

Mom leaned stiffly against the doorjamb. "I'm all ears."

"I — I — " A million thoughts swam around in my head. I was humiliated. I was embarrassed. All I could say was a feeble, "I'm sorry, Mom."

"I accept the apology," Mom replied. "But a rule is a rule, Kristy, and I'm grounding you for the weekend."

"Grounding?"

"To your bedroom, except to use the bathroom. Until Monday. And I am removing your TV."

I wanted to scream. This was so unfair. I didn't plan for this to happen. I didn't sneak Bart into the house. I hadn't even been expecting him.

"It wasn't my fault!" I said as I bounded out of the den.

I clomped up the stairs to my dungeon. With each step, I thought of a new way to destroy Bart Taylor.

CHAPTER 8

Boiling in oil.

Hanging by the toes.

The rack.

Being force-fed steamed lima beans.

Each torture method had the same basic flaw. It was too kind to Bart.

How could he do this to me? The thought was like a throbbing sore in my brain. It kept me awake that night.

I hadn't asked for any of this to happen. Bart was the reason for my prison sentence. Bart had ruined my family life.

Bart, my pushy, thoughtless, former-sort-of-boyfriend-who-wanted-to-be-a-real-boyfriend-but-is-now-dead-meat-instead.

And then, after I thought the night couldn't possibly have been worse, the Mets lost (I listened to the game on my clock radio).

Boy, did my room look small in the dark. Tiny. As I lay there, gazing at the four walls, they seemed to be crowding in. I thought about my activities for the upcoming weekend. Reading. Thinking. Reaching for the phone. Maybe taking a walk to my closet every once in awhile. Jogging to the bathroom.

What fun. I would emerge on Monday, shriveled and pale. Blinking in the unfamiliar sunlight. Baffled by the outside world.

Like E. T.

E. T. T. Extraterrestrial Thomas.

And what about Saturday's tournament? What was I going to tell Karen and Andrew and David Michael? Not to mention all the other neighborhood kids. They were all counting on me.

I could just hear them screaming. Crying. Holding a protest march outside my window. Chanting, "Free Kristy! Free Kristy!"

Fat chance.

Abby would have to take down the records all by herself. Ugh. Then I had an even worse thought: what if she had some strange allergic reaction? What if that many kids were just too much for one girl to handle? I could see her collapsing to the ground, helpless.

Sunday's headlines would read NEIGHBORHOOD BABY-SITTING ENTREPRENEUR EMBROILED IN KISSING SCANDAL: IMPLICATED IN FRIEND'S CRITICAL COLLAPSE!

Of all the horrible moments of my life, this

had to be right there on top of the list.

I turned onto my stomach. I tried to think peaceful, sleepy thoughts.

The last image I remember before fading into sleep was of Bart, dressed in turn-of-the-century clothes, tied to a train trestle while an approaching steam engine smoked in the distance. Chugging ever closer.

Saturday morning I awoke at seven-thirty. Or I should say I was awakened, by Andrew screaming "I want waffles" at the top of his lungs.

Ha. Normally I'd slump downstairs and rustle up the morning grub. But not today. Mom or Watson would have to do it. They weren't going to have Kristy to kick around for awhile.

See? If you look close enough, you can find a bright side to everything.

I still wasn't sure how I was supposed to eat during this cruel incarceration. (Like that word? Alone for two whole days in a room with a thesaurus, I learned a lot of cool prison-related words. Here are some synonyms for jail: *gaol*, *hoosegow*, *the slammer*, and *the clink*.)

I also hadn't been told whether I was allowed to use my phone. However, I had an excellent idea what my mom's answer to that question would be.

The problem was, I desperately needed to call Abby.

Well, as long as I hadn't actually asked, then no one had officially said no. Right?

When I heard grown-up footsteps thumping downstairs, I sat up. If I was going to call, this was the best time to do it.

Unlike Claudia's, my phone is only an extension. Carefully I lifted the receiver off the hook and held my fingers over the buttons.

" . . . we really took a beating on those growth funds, and I'm not bullish these days . . ."

Oops. Watson-talk. I put the receiver down gently.

About five minutes later, I heard Watson shuffle downstairs.

I grabbed the phone and tapped Abby's number. After about ten rings, I heard, "Haaarrbbbsh?"

"Abby?" I said.

"Hrrrm . . . chhhk . . ." Abby cleared her throat. "Who is this?"

"Me, Kristy!"

"Am I late or something?"

"Nope."

"Good. It feels like minus one in the morning. See you in a few hours."

"Don't hang up!" I quickly told Abby what

had happened with Bart and how I'd been punished.

Her response? "All riiiight, Kristy! Kissing Bandit! Whoooo!"

It wasn't what I had expected.

"You don't understand," I said. "We promised the kids a tournament. Can you do it alone?"

Silence.

"Abby, are you still there?" I asked.

"I think I'm about to have a nervous breakdown."

"Don't. Look, we can figure something out."

"I can call the kids and cancel," Abby suggested. "But I'll be itching the rest of the day from all their voodoo-doll pins."

"I have a better idea," I said. "Gather them at my house, just the way we planned. Then I can help you."

"Kristy, look, I know your room is pretty big — " Abby began.

"Not in my room, in the yard! I'll coach you from my window."

"Can you do that?"

"I'll still be in my room, right? That was what — "

I heard my door open. "Uh, excuse me?" my mom's voice said.

" 'Bye!" I blurted out, quickly slamming the receiver down.

Mom was walking toward me with a breakfast tray — cereal, toast with jam, and orange juice. "No phone calls, Kristy," she said sternly, shaking her head. "In or out. This isn't meant to be pleasure time."

"Okay, Mom, sorry." I smiled. "The waiter service sure is good, though."

"Well, you see, you can find a silver lining in every cloud."

Just what I would have said.

Jug. Can. Cooler. Coop. Pokey. I ran my finger down a page of my thesaurus.

House arrest.

That was the best one. That described exactly my plight.

Kristy Thomas, under house arrest. Political prisoner. (Okay, I'm going overboard. But it does sound good.)

Around noon, I heard a tap at my window. I looked out and saw Abby standing in the driveway, holding a spiral notebook with one hand, rearing back as if to throw a pebble with her other hand.

I opened the window and discovered it was warm, sunny, and breezy outside. "Hi!" I called out.

"Reporting for action," Abby said. "What should I do?"

"Mom and Watson already know about the tournament. The kids have been talking about it all week. Just ring the bell and say you're ready. Then bring the kids here. Piece of cake."

Abby followed my instructions. In a few minutes, Karen, David Michael, and Andrew came racing onto the lawn, with Emily toddling along behind.

"Kisss-teeee!" Emily screamed, reaching as if she could pull me down.

"Rapunzel, Rapunzel, let down your hair!" Karen shouted up to me.

"Kristy's being punished, Kristy's being punished," David Michael sang.

I stayed calm. I was not going to let any teasing get me down. "Okay, guys, it's a nice day, so I thought we could do a few athletic events — "

"Kristy and Bart, sitting in a tree," David Michael chimed in, "K-I-S-S-I-N-G!"

How did he know? That little sneak. He was probably spying on us the night before.

I kept my cool. "First event," I said, "is how many kids can tickle David Michael at the same time."

"Yeaaaaa!" They all ran after him, including Abby.

Then they settled down to business. First was the Backward Jump contest, which was won by . . .

Linny Papadakis!

Yes, as soon as the festivities were underway, the rest of the neighborhood piled into our yard — Linny and Hannie, Bill and Melody, Scott and Timmy.

Abby did a great job. She measured everyone's jump distances, wrote down the records, calmed a fight, made the kids laugh. (Except for Andrew. Everyone jumped farther than he did.) Then she conducted a Keeping-a-Volleyball-in-the-Air event, which lasted thirty-three hits.

Andrew didn't fare too well with that one, either.

Next, Timmy Hsu wanted to do a Long-Distance Off-the-Porch Leap.

"A feat of great danger and skill!" I shouted. "Let's line up for the challenge."

"All kids who have had eggs for breakfast first!" Abby announced.

"Me! Me!" shouted Scott and Timmy.

"Pancakes next!" I said.

"Yyyyyes!" cried Linny.

"How about liverwurst with onions?" I called down.

"Ewwwwww!"

I was about to say something else ridiculous,

when I noticed I was being watched.

By Mom. She was standing just under my window, with her arms tightly crossed. "Ahem," she said.

"I'm in my room," I reminded her.

"I see I need to be a bit more explicit with you, Kristy," Mom replied. "You are not to speak to anyone on the phone *or* through your window."

"Yes, Mom." I sank back onto my bed, away from the window.

I could tell when Mom was gone, because all the kids started giggling.

I couldn't talk? What a horrible fate. What was I supposed to do? Just sit and rot, with no human contact?

Bing! Another idea.

I popped back up into the window and waved until I had everyone's attention. Then I continued to coach.

By pantomiming.

I demonstrated the proper form for the jump, then pointed to the porch. I cheered the kids on by clapping.

It was the clapping that brought Mom back.

"Correction," she said. "You may not *be seen* by anyone through your window. Do you understand?"

Grumbling, I pulled my shades down.

As I heard my mom's footsteps walking back

down the driveway, I thought of a great idea for an event.

Hmmm . . .

I wrote it down on a sheet of looseleaf paper. Carefully I folded it in half lengthwise. Then I folded it a few more times, into a perfect airplane shape.

I pulled back the shades ever so slightly. With a flick of the wrist, I sent it flying onto the lawn.

Not one person saw me. And that's the truth.

CHAPTER 9

As it turned out, the Saturday tournament was the high point of the weekend. Everything afterward was downhill.

Mom managed to find one of the airplane messages and was not amused. I'm surprised she didn't clap me in irons. (That's an expression I remember from one of the gazillion books I ended up reading over the weekend. It means "put me in chains.")

Charlie and Sam both knocked on my door, laughing, wanting every detail of what I'd done. Instead, I unleashed my secret weapon. I told Charlie I knew he'd brought Sarah to the house when no one was home, and if he ever bothered me again I'd tell Mom.

That made quick work of him.

After the neighborhood kids and Abby left, I paced around the room like a caged animal. Then I grabbed every book off my shelf that I hadn't read, and I began going through them.

I became so tired of reading silently, I started reading aloud. I was in the middle of a wild passage from *Shiloh*, using a booming voice and an accent to boot, when I heard a giggle from outside the doorway.

It was David Michael, eavesdropping.

"Go away, you sneaky little rat!" I cried.

"Who're you talking to, Kristy?" David Michael taunted me. "Your *boyfriend?*"

"David Michael, when I'm finally out of here, you will be so sorry — "

"Kristyyyyyy!" Watson called out from downstairs.

Thump. Thump. Thump. Thump. Upstairs he came.

I listened to my nine thousandth lecture of the weekend. This time, I was told I could not talk through the door.

I went back to silent reading until my eyes felt numb.

I listened to tapes.

I drew.

I napped.

I did situps. Pushups. Jumping jacks.

By dinnertime, I, Kristy Thomas, was out of ideas. All I could think about was eating.

At six o'clock Mom entered. With spinach croquettes.

My appetite flew out the window. I could not believe my mother, who once loved me, was forcing these foul-smelling, putrid globules on me. I seriously considered chucking them out the window.

Longest Distance, Yucky-Dinner Hurl.

I went to bed that night with a growling stomach. At least I could look forward to sleep.

Or so I thought.

I was wide awake. Flying.

I read some more. I turned out the light and counted sheep. I counted fly balls. I counted flying sheep. I tried to focus on one area without blinking.

Nothing worked.

And then I thought about Bart.

I won't even mention some of the things that shot through my mind. They made boiling in oil seem kind in comparison.

The longer my insomnia continued, the more diabolical my thoughts became.

Somehow that made me happier. I finally managed to doze off.

The next morning, however, Mom practically had to pry me out of bed with a crowbar.

Then, of course, I had to face Sunday. I do believe it was the absolute worst day of my life. The pits. I ran out of books to read, so I made up songs, usually with lyrics along the lines of, "Row, row, row your boat, roughly over Bart's head; merrily, merrily, merrily, merrily, look out, Bart, you're dead."

To pass the time, I constructed some of my own puzzles. These word changes, for example:

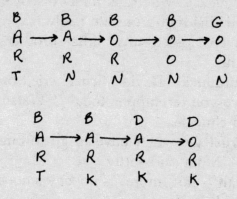

Do you think I was being a little hard on Bart?

I know, I know. I was obsessed. Immature. Childish. Morbid.

But you try being locked in your room for two days and see how it feels.

I thought Sunday would never end. But when it did, I had made a big decision.

I knew exactly what I was going to say to Bart Taylor.

On Monday morning, I practically flew out my bedroom door. Freedom! What a feeling. Things I had taken for granted seemed so glorious. I chose my own cereal. I saw the interior of the refrigerator. I used the downstairs bathroom.

I felt like Jimmy Stewart at the end of *It's a Wonderful Life*, when he finally discovers how fantastic his humdrum life really is.

I even kissed my little brother good morning.

"Yuuuuuck!" David Michael cried out.

"My, you're chipper today," Watson said with a chuckle.

"I trust we won't have to go through this again," Mom said softly.

"Yeah, no more smoochy-smoochies," David Michael said.

Charlie and Sam thought that was hysterical.

Me? I laughed, too. I didn't care. I had big plans for the evening.

To tell you the truth, I had never been so happy to go to school in my life. When I sat with Abby on the bus, I might as well have been on a plane to Disney World.

"Are you okay?" Abby asked.

"Fine," I replied cheerfully.

"Did your mom make you quit the BSC?"

"Nope. My punishment is over."

"I guess you'll have to, you know, do stuff at Bart's from now on, huh?"

"Whaaaaaat?"

"You know, since your house is off-limits now."

"Abby, it's not like that!"

"Okay, okay. I'll mind my own business."

Even Abby's comments didn't bother me. Nothing did that day. School, the BSC meeting, dinner. Everything went smoothly. I even managed to think of an alternate plan for our *Record Wreckers* show, in case it rained. We'd have it in Mary Anne's barn (if her parents agreed).

Around seven-thirty, when I knew Bart would be sitting down to the pre-game ceremonies of another televised spring training game, I went into my room and shut the door.

Then I tapped out his phone number.

"Hello?" Good. It was Bart.

"Hey. Haven't heard from you in awhile."

"Kristy! Hi! Wow, I tried to call you Saturday, but your mom picked up."

"Oh, what did you guys talk about?"

Bart let out a deep breath. "Not much. I mean, I kind of hung up when I heard her voice."

"Well, it's just as well. She wouldn't have let you talk to me, anyway. I was quarantined for the weekend."

"Oh, no. You were sick?"

"Nope. Grounded. Put in my room for two

whole days. All alone. Ignored. Like the crazy wife in *Jane Eyre*."

"Who?"

"It's a book, Bart. One of the many I read over the weekend. That's about all I could do."

"Oh, wow, Kristy. Look, I'm really sorry. I guess we kind of got carried away."

"We?"

"Well, yeah. I mean, I couldn't believe your parents came home so early. I almost died."

I think that was what Bart said. I'm not sure. My brain was sparking. Misfiring. I could barely see straight.

"*We?*" I repeated. "*We* didn't get carried away. You did! I was all set to watch TV alone. Did I invite you? No. Did you ask? No. You could have warned me about your plans when we were at the Argo!"

"I didn't know then," Bart replied. "And I didn't think dropping over would be such a big deal. If I had known about that no-boyfriend rule, I wouldn't have stayed. Why didn't you tell me?"

"I thought you just wanted to watch the game. I thought you were coming over as . . . as a baseball fan. Not as a boyfriend!"

"Well, I'm not two people, Kristy."

"What's that supposed to mean?"

"I am a baseball fan. But I am also your boyfriend."

"Oh, really? Well, dream on, Bart Man. Starting right now, you are history."

"But — but — "

Click.

Done.

I let out a loud whoop. I punched the air in triumph.

What a relief. I'd said exactly what I wanted to say. I wasn't going to have to worry about Bart anymore.

Boy, did I feel rotten.

CHAPTER 10

Tuesday

Most Arguments Broken up.
Most Crying Faces Wiped.
Most Hurt Feelings Comforted.
Quickest Exit from a Job.
Longest-Lasting Headache.
Kristy, can we include some baby-sitter records? Think about it ...

Poor Stacey. She had been looking forward to sitting for Matt and Haley Braddock. She couldn't wait to be a part of *Record Wreckers*. She thought it would be "so cute."

Even when Tuesday turned out to be cool and cloudy, Stacey was determined to take the kids outside. She showed up for her job with a clipboard, a stopwatch, a whistle, and a stack of papers divided into columns marked CATEGORY, RECORD, and RECORD HOLDER. She wore a brand-new designer baseball cap, but brought along a slightly grubby one, just in case it rained. (Team player or not, she's still Stacey.)

A moment after she rang the bell, the door flew open. "Staceyyyyyyy!" Haley screamed at the top of her lungs. "Guess what? We have a whole bag of potatoes!"

"Uh, that's nice," Stacey replied.

Haley is nine. Matt, who's seven, was jumping up and down, gesturing with his hands and fingers. (Matt was born profoundly deaf, which means he cannot hear at all. We BSC members have learned a bit of American Sign Language, which is what Matt uses to communicate.)

Stacey waved hi to Matt and tried to figure out what he was saying.

Mrs. Braddock bustled into the front parlor.

"Stacey, I'm glad it's you and not me," she said with a laugh. "I don't mind if these events are messy, but do clean up. And use your judgment. No plate-throwing contests, if you know what I mean. I'm meeting Mr. Braddock in town and we'll be back around eight . . ."

She gave a flurry of instructions and bolted.

"Let me guess," Stacey said. "You want to make the world's largest potato salad?"

Haley rolled her eyes. "Are you kidding? What about, like, big restaurants? They make way bigger salads than we could make."

"Good point."

"We're going to throw them!" Haley said.

"Oh."

That came out more like "ew." Cleaning up smashed potatoes? Stacey's enthusiasm was already fading.

Haley was gazing outside at the dark clouds. "Let's go before it rains."

Matt began signing something. Haley interpreted, "He says he hopes it doesn't rain the day of the show."

"Tell him not to worry," Stacey said. "Mary Anne said we could hold it in her barn." (Wasn't I clever to think of asking her? Thank you, thank you.)

Stacey helped Matt tote the sack outside. They dropped it on the deck, near the back door. (The Braddocks have a small deck with a picnic table, and beyond it a long, narrow yard.)

Matt disappeared into the garage. He emerged a moment later with a baseball bat and laid it on the ground in front of Stacey.

"The bat will be the line," Haley announced.

She and Matt quickly negotiated something in sign language, and Matt let out a cheer.

"He gets to throw first," Haley grumped.

Well, those must have been some potatoes. Most of them didn't even break when they hit the ground. Just thudded. By the time Haley and Matt reached the bottom of the sack, the backyard looked as if it was infested with strange little brownish-gray rodents.

"Hey, cool!" called a voice from the driveway. "Our turn."

Stacey turned to see Nicky, Vanessa, Margo, and Claire Pike running toward her. On Nicky's back was a bulging backpack.

"Hi!" Stacey greeted them. "Guess what we're doing."

"We know," Vanessa said. "Haley called us."

Haley nodded. "Also the Arnolds. And I mentioned it to Jenny Prezzioso and Jamie Newton, but they're little, so they probably won't come."

Nicky dropped his backpack on the ground.

"Give me one!" he shouted, practically grabbing a potato from Matt.

"Me first!" Vanessa cried.

"Nickyyyyyy," Margo said, pulling a bunch of bananas from the backpack. "You bruised them!"

Making loud pig snorts, Claire ran into the yard among the potatoes. "I'm hunting truffles!" she yelled.

She was beaned from behind by a flying spud.

"Owwwwww!" Claire fell to the ground, whimpering.

Stacey ran to her. Potatoes rained around them like mutant hailstones.

"Out of the way!" shouted Nicky.

"Waaaaahhhhhh!" wailed Claire.

"Can I take my shoes off?" asked Margo.

Stacey's head was spinning. She scooped up Claire and took her out of the line of fire.

As she stood in the driveway, examining Claire's head for bumps, she spotted Carolyn and Marilyn Arnold barreling into the backyard. (They, by the way, are eight-year-old identical twins.)

"Us next!" Carolyn screamed.

Eight kids. One baby-sitter. A sack of potatoes. An injury.

And a whole afternoon of record-setting ahead.

Stacey's stomach was sinking fast.

Wild laughter rang out from across the yard. Margo Pike was now sitting against the house, peeling a banana with her bare feet.

"Aren't you cold?" Stacey asked.

Margo shrugged. Claire and the twins were doubled over, howling. Holding the peeled banana between her toes, Margo offered it to Carolyn.

"Gross!" Carolyn cried.

"I'll eat it!" Nicky volunteered.

But Margo squeezed too hard, and the banana fell into the grass in two pieces.

More screaming.

"I'll do another one," Margo offered. "I'm going to do three whole bunches. A world record!"

"Let me try!" Marilyn said.

Stacey girded her loins. (That was another phrase I read during my weekend of punishment. I'm not sure what it means, but soldiers did it before battle.)

Still in mid-gird, she spotted Mrs. Prezzioso and Mrs. Newton walking up the driveway. They were carrying their babies in Snuglis, and they were hand-in-hand with their four-year-olds — Jenny P and Jamie N.

"Stacey," Mrs. Prezzioso said, "we're so grateful you agreed to take care of Jenny and Jamie for the afternoon. Mrs. Newton and I have been meaning to coo over our babies with a cappuccino for such a long time."

Squealing with delight, Jamie and Jenny ran into the backyard.

Agreed?

Stacey was dumbfounded. "Uh-huh," she mumbled.

She forced her gaping mouth shut. She managed to smile. She waved to the moms as they left for their coo-and-cappuccino date.

But inside her head, a major temper tantrum raged.

"Watch ooooout!" shouted Nicky.

A skateboard shot by Stacey. On it was a wrapped-up single roll of toilet paper, which tumbled off. Nicky and Matt, the launchers, were giggling in the garage.

"It's a race!" Nicky said. "Whoever lets it go the longest without dropping the toilet paper wins the world record!"

Stacey stepped to the side. She could see Haley coaching Jamie on the fine art of potato throwing. Marilyn was barefoot now, sitting next to Margo and making mush out of a banana.

Carolyn and Vanessa emerged from the house with two family packs of string cheese. They dumped the packs on the picnic table and began unwrapping the individual cheeses.

"Wait a second," Stacey said. "Why don't you just take enough to eat?"

Carolyn rolled her eyes. "We're not *eating* them."

Before Stacey could reply, she heard a bloodcurdling scream behind her.

She spun around. Jenny had collapsed onto the ground in sobs. "I'll never throw it far enough!" she screamed.

Haley shrugged. "I keep telling her she's doing great."

"It's not as far as Haley!" Jenny wailed.

Jamie wound up and threw. His potato went sideways, plopped to the ground, and rolled onto the driveway.

Right in the path of the skateboard race.

The skateboard hit it. The toilet paper toppled off. Nicky yelled "Do over!"

And Jamie burst into tears to match Jenny's. "I can't I can't I can't!" he yelled.

From the garage, Nicky called out, "We'll show you how!"

He and Matt raced over, scooping up potatoes on the way.

"No!" Haley said. "You're not allowed!"

"Why not?" Nicky asked.

"Because you've had your chance," Haley

replied. "Give the younger kids a turn."

"You can't stop us!" Nicky said.

Matt threw a potato clear into the next yard.

"Yes, I can, and I say that doesn't count," Haley retorted. "I *invented* the potato throw."

"Waaaah!" cried Jenny and Jamie. Stacey lifted them both.

"Fourteen!" Margo chimed in. "Haley, do you have any more bananas inside?"

Stacey glanced over and saw Margo and Marilyn surrounded by peels and naked bananas.

On the picnic table, Carolyn and Vanessa were each tying together strings of cheese, racing against each other to make the world's longest cheese rope.

Stacey's head was spinning. The yard was going to be a trash bin by the time the Braddocks came home. "I know!" she said to Jenny and Jamie. "The Most Banana Peels Tossed into a Garbage Can."

"Okay," Jamie said with a pout.

Stacey quickly lowered the two four-year-olds to the ground. Then she fetched a can from the garage.

Jenny and Jamie gleefully picked up peels and started throwing. Jenny managed two and Jamie three. Then Margo and Claire joined. And Marilyn. And Nicky.

Jenny and Jamie gave up and skulked away. Stacey chased after them. Matt ran inside to get more bananas. A neighbor peeked over the fence, holding a potato, and asked, "Is this yours?"

Margo shouted, "That was my throw!"

"Liar!" Nicky yelled.

"Stacey! Carolyn took one of my string cheeses!" Vanessa said.

Stacey kind of short-circuited right then. She doesn't remember much about the rest of the day.

Except that she went right to sleep after dinner. And vowed never to baby-sit again. Ever.

Don't worry. It lasted about three days. She should have added one more record to her request in the BSC notebook.

World's Shortest Baby-sitting Retirement.

CHAPTER 11

*R*rrrinng!

The phone woke me Saturday morning. Yawning, I rolled around and reached for the receiver.

I quickly stopped myself. I had almost forgotten. Answering the phone was strictly off-limits.

Any call could be Bart. I would not allow him the satisfaction of reaching me so easily.

All week I had instructed everyone in my family: if Bart called, tell him I wasn't home.

No one ever had to.

It was now five days after the breakup, and Bart had not called.

Not once. Not even one suspicious hang-up had occurred (I asked every day).

"Kristyyyyyy!" David Michael shouted from downstairs. "It's your *boyfriend!*"

My heart stopped. I felt as if a large prehistoric reptile had sat on my chest.

I ran to the door, flung it open, and whispered down the stairs, "Tell him I'm not home!"

"He knows you are," David Michael replied. "He says he loves you and wants to take you out and kiss you and buy you flowers."

"Whaaaaat?"

Oh, this was low. I mean, apologizing is one thing. But giving me the silent treatment for a whole week, then calling out of the blue and saying all those private things to my seven-year-old brother?

Despicable.

I ran back into my room. I could hear David Michael scampering upstairs.

Before picking up the phone, I stopped. I pictured Bart on the other end. Looking all scrunch-eyed at his phone. Missing me. Feeling sorry. Wanting to take me out and buy me flowers. Wanting it so badly that he couldn't keep his mouth shut to David Michael.

Typical Bart, I thought. Exactly the way he was at the movie theater. And at my house Friday night. Wanting so much to go from sort-of-boyfriend to Boyfriend-with-a-capital-B, but not knowing how to ask.

Or even realizing he should ask.

Maybe he wanted to ask now.

I sighed. It could be worse. He could be calling up to yell at me. Hang up on me the way I'd hung up on him.

I would listen. Let him speak. At least hear him out.

I grabbed the receiver. "Okay, talk fast."

"Excuse me? Hello?"

It was a totally unfamiliar, female voice.

"That's just my little sister," Charlie's voice cut in. "Hang up, dorkface."

"Oh! Uh, okay," I mumbled. "Sorry."

David Michael had lied. *Sarah* had called, to talk to Charlie.

"Hooooo ha ha ha ha!" David Michael was whooping with laughter outside my room.

"You creep!" I flew out the door and chased him downstairs. But he had had a big head start. And it's practically impossible to catch someone in a house our size.

"You're not worth it!" I shouted.

I stormed back upstairs, mumbling under my breath.

To be honest, I wasn't really thinking about David Michael. I was thinking about Bart.

I couldn't help it. My feelings were like a big bowl of spaghetti with clam sauce, all twisted and mixed up with stuff I couldn't digest.

Nothing made sense. Bart was a jerk. I broke

up with him. I should have felt great. I should have been able to forget about him. Period.

So why was I mad at him for not calling?

And why had I been so excited when I thought he *had* called?

Why was I so ready to forgive him for being a jerk?

I had to talk to someone. Someone who would know what to do. Someone who had a real boyfriend. Like Stacey or Mary Anne.

Right. Duh. I could just picture the look on their faces. That *Kristy-can't-understand-anything-that's-not-sports* look.

Then I thought of Jessi and Mal. They'd both had sort-of boyfriends. True, they're both eleven, but so what? At least they wouldn't laugh at me.

I tapped Jessi's number on the phone. Her dad answered, then went to find her.

"Hi, Kristy, what's up?" Jessi asked.

"If I tell you something, will you promise to keep it a secret?" I asked.

"Sure," Jessi replied.

I told her everything that had happened. Everything I was feeling.

She listened patiently, then let out a deep sigh. "Wow. You sound so upset. But I'm not sure I know what to do, Kristy."

"Well, you liked Quint and Curtis, right?

And even, you know, kissed and stuff?"

Ugh. I could barely listen to myself sound so dumb.

"Oh, it's so nice that you thought of me," Jessi replied. "But, you know, Quint was long distance, and we sort of drifted apart. And Curtis and I aren't that serious or anything. Why don't you ask Mary Anne? She's your best friend."

"She's had a boyfriend for a million years," I said. "I feel so stupid asking her."

"Asking Mary Anne? No way!" Jessi reassured me. "She'd be upset if she found out about this and knew you *didn't* talk to her."

"Yeah . . . I guess you're right."

I said good-bye and put my finger on the receiver hook. Thomas, do not be a chicken, I told myself. If you can't count on Mary Anne, you can't count on anyone. Then I took ten deep breaths and tapped out the Spiers' number.

"Hello?" her dad's voice said.

"Oh, hi, it's Kristy. I guess Mary Anne's not there. Nothing important. I'll talk to her tomorrow."

"Uh, Kristy? She *is* here. Hang on."

Gulp.

I did some of my own loin-girding. I was going to present the problem. Coolly. Maturely. In detail, so Mary Anne would know how to help.

"Hello?" Mary Anne said.

"Hi, Mary Anne . . ."

I couldn't believe it. Tears were sliding down my cheeks. My nose was starting to run. I had to snuffle like a pig.

"Kristy, what's wrong? Are you okay?"

"Yeah. I mean, no. I mean, Mary Anne, I — I hate Bart but I want him to call me and he wants to be my boyfriend and I guess I want that too because I think he really likes me but I'm not sure because he does the wrong things and sometimes makes me feel weird and I'm not sure I'm ready for what he wants me to be and I feel like such a total stupid nerd!"

"Whoa, whoa, Kristy," Mary Anne said. "Say it again, slowly, as if I'm just learning English."

I could picture the smile on her face and it was warm and understanding, not mocking. I started again. I told her exactly how I felt, slowly.

When I finished, I could hear Mary Anne sigh. "That's a tough one. You and Bart had such a great friendship. Can you just go back to the way it was?"

"But he wants it to be more, Mary Anne,"

I said. "And I don't know, maybe it *should* be more. I mean, we're not little kids. Do you think I'm being babyish?"

"It doesn't sound like you're ready for Bart to be your boyfriend," Mary Anne said.

"But I'm thirteen!"

Mary Anne was silent for a moment. "Kristy, how old were you when you learned how to walk?"

"Nine months," I replied. "Or nine-and-a-half. I forget."

"I was fifteen months old," Mary Anne said. "My dad said you used to bop Claudia and me with a doll because we could only crawl."

I laughed. "I probably stunted your growth."

"Don't you see, Kristy? Claudia and I weren't ready to walk when you were. But eventually we learned, and now who cares? I never chose my own clothes until seventh grade, and Stacey probably fussed over the style of her diapers. People don't do everything at the same rate."

"Yeah, but how do you know when to start?" I asked. "Maybe you have to just jump in. Like a sport. You can't hit a baseball unless you pick up a bat and try."

"Yeah, but if you feel like you're being forced to bat, you're not going to do well. Or enjoy it. Right?"

"Yup," I said. "You have to want it. That's rule number one."

"Do you want it?" Mary Anne asked.

"Want what?"

"Want Bart to be your boyfriend?"

"I don't know! That's what I'm trying to say!"

"Because if you're not ready, you're not ready, Kristy. Ten, thirteen, fifteen, thirty — it doesn't matter what age. Nobody should do anything that doesn't feel right. Ever."

I was about to talk, but the words caught in my throat.

All the tangles and knots in my head were loosening up. Unraveling.

Mary Anne was right. The funny thing was, she wasn't telling me anything I didn't already know.

But somehow, I needed to hear it from someone else.

"Kristy? You really should talk to Bart," Mary Anne said softly.

"I know," I replied. "I will. Thanks, Mary Anne. You've been a big help."

Even as I hung up, I was thinking of the words I was going to say to Bart.

It was going to be the hardest conversation of my life.

I desided somthing. You geys ~~definitle~~ ~~difein defanit~~ realy take me for granted. *Sundae*

I may have lousey speling. I may not no how to eat write. I may dress funy somtimes, and make two many jokes at BSC meetings.

But evry ounce in a while I can do things even the grate Kristy can't think of . . .

No comment.

Claudia can think whatever she wants. She's entitled.

Even when she's wrong.

I suppose I should explain. Claudia sat for Jenny Prezzioso on Sunday, the day after my long talk with Mary Anne.

Sitting for the Prezziosos can be a trying experience. Don't misunderstand me. I don't mean to put them down. I love all our clients. I treat them equally and never play favorites.

Well, I try as hard as I can. But let's face it, some families make it a little bit harder than others.

Claudia wore a bowling shirt with the name *Ralph* sewn over the front pocket, and matching loose rayon pants, gathered at the waist with a leather strip. She'd pinned her hair with a barrette in the shape of two bowling pins.

Mrs. Prezzioso greeted her with a weird expression at the front door. "Are you in a league?" she asked.

At first Claudia didn't know what she was talking about. "A what? Oh, my clothes? No, it's just, you know, a look."

"I *love* it," Mrs. P. said with a tone of voice she might have used if Claud were wearing a cheese jumpsuit. "How . . . retro."

She smiled, adjusting the pleats on her brand-new wool skirt.

I have never seen Jenny's parents look casual. You'd think they lived in a TV commercial. (Actually, Jenny's baby sister, Andrea, *has* been in commercials. She's a professional model.)

Mr. and Mrs. Prezzioso talked with Claudia awhile. They all cooed over Andrea, who was in a playpen by the living room piano.

Then, as Mr. and Mrs. P. left, they called good-bye to Jenny.

" 'Bye . . ." answered a tiny, glum voice from the other side of the living room.

Claud looked around. She noticed one of the sofa cushions was out of place. Two feet were poking out the side.

"Hiding?" Claudia asked.

"Did you bring a Kid-Kit?" was Jenny's greeting.

"Well, no," Claudia said. "I thought you and some of the other kids might want to set some records."

The sofa cushion fell to the floor. Jenny sat up, arms folded. "Go home and get it!"

Claudia laughed. "You don't sound too happy."

"I hate setting records. It's boring!"

"Okay. We can think of other things to do."

But Jenny wasn't finished. "We're too little

for records. All the big kids set records!"

"Jenny, who's 'we'?" Claudia asked.

"Me and Jamie. And Claire. But she's five."

Claudia had read Stacey's notebook entry from Tuesday. She remembered that Jenny and Jamie had been frustrated with the older kids. And I had told her that Andrew had been in a funk since Saturday. (He had taken his long-jump defeat hard, and afterward Linny broke his spaghetti-sucking record.)

"It's not fair, is it?" Claudia said. "All those big kids hogging the records."

"Yeah!"

Claudia sat silently for a moment. Jenny can be moody and cranky, and the last thing Claudia wanted to do was spend the afternoon taking orders from a four-year-old.

"Why don't we set some records of our own?" she finally asked.

"I said *no!*"

"Without any big kids," Claudia pressed on. "A special day just for four-year-olds records. We'll see if Jamie wants to do it, too."

Jenny thought about it for a moment. "Four *and* five," she said. "So Claire can come, too."

"Great. We'll ask her parents if she can come over."

Claudia bundled Andrea up and put her in a stroller. Then she helped Jenny into a warm coat.

The moment they stepped outside, Jenny was twitchy with excitement. "If I sit on your shoulders, I can throw a potato ten miles!"

"Let's stick to things the big kids wouldn't try to challenge."

Jenny giggled. "Silly, they wouldn't sit on your shoulders!"

Well, Claud was in luck. Mr. and Mrs. Pike were happy to let Claire out. Ditto with the Newtons and Jamie.

On the way back to Jenny's house, the kids all started singing at the top of their lungs. First the Barney song, about twenty times. Then "Rubber Ducky." Then "Captain Vegetable."

On Jenny's front lawn, they acted out silly versions of *Mary Poppins* songs, such as "I Love to Burp," instead of "I Love to Laugh."

Claudia sat on the stoop, laughing. Beside her in the stroller, Andrea stared, fascinated.

They were so cute, Claudia thought. Free and happy, doing stuff the older kids would just roll their eyes at.

Blink. The lightbulb in Claudia's head popped on.

"Who's ready for a speed-singing event?" she called out.

"Meeeeeee!"

"Okay, when I count to three, everybody

sing the Barney song as fast as you can." Claudia pulled back her coat sleeve and looked at her watch. "One . . . two . . . three!"

"Iloveyouyoulovemerabblefrabbafamawama," a babble of voices rang out. Then screams of "I finished first!" and "No, I did!" and "You cheated!"

Oops.

"Rule change!" Claudia called out. "We better do this one at a time."

(I could have told her that from the start.)

She timed them separately. Jenny won. Then she timed three more speed-singing songs, until each kid won.

Afterward Claudia had to change Andrea's diaper, so everyone went inside. Claire and Jenny began playing catch with one of Andrea's plastic diapers.

That was when Claire had her brainstorm. "A diaper toss!" she squealed. "Longest throw wins!"

"Yeaaaaaa!"

Funny. All Claudia could think about was Dawn Schafer. Dawn is incredibly environmentally conscious. She always hated the idea of disposable diapers. Wasting them for a game? She'd have a fit.

Quietly, as if Dawn were listening, Claud said, "Okay, but we'll use only one."

The diaper toss was a big success. You had to throw it just right, or it would open and fan out.

Next was the Cookie Monster stuffed doll catch.

And the Thomas the Tank Engine train race on parallel Brio tracks (an indoor event).

And the longest K'nex contraption that didn't fall apart of its own weight.

Claudia recorded every event. She knew none of the big kids would go near these records.

Boy, was Claud proud of herself. She called me that night to suggest that Andrew might want to participate in the same sort of thing.

Which I had intended anyway.

But I was still grateful.

CHAPTER 13

"READY?" I asked through my bullhorn.

Next to me, Stacey leaped about a foot off the picnic bench. "Can't you warn me, Kristy?"

"Yeaaaaa!" shouted Linny, Bill, Vanessa, and David Michael, as they lined up at one end of Mary Anne's backyard.

It was Tuesday afternoon, and we were having our first rehearsal for the *Record Wreckers* show. All the kids had shown up, wild with excitement.

The show was going to happen that Saturday. Why so soon? Because the kids were dying of anticipation, for one thing. Also because it was the only day Mary Anne's yard was free.

Which meant we had four days to send invitations, rehearse the show, and write the book.

Stacey had been busily collating all our

looseleaf sheets (except for Bart's, which he still had). Her job was to figure out a format for the book, and Mary Anne was to type it and print it on her parents' computer.

I waited until Stacey's hands were over her ears. Then I shouted into the bullhorn: "GET SET . . . SPIN!"

Vanessa began twirling across the yard. The rest of the kids cheered as loudly as they could. Except Linny. He was staring skeptically.

"That shouldn't count!" Linny said as she crossed the finish line. "I could do much better than that!"

Vanessa smirked at him. "Linny, Linny, don't be a ninny!"

"Hey, unsportsmanlike conduct!" Linny shot back. "She should be disqualified, the little nerd!"

Mary Anne, the great peacemaker, ran over to break up the fight. The other kids were gathering around us, shouting all at once:

"Potato throw next!"

"No, the skateboard toilet paper event!"

"Longest burp!"

"Backward jump!"

I gave Stacey a Look. I think we were both wondering why on Earth we'd ever agreed to do this.

Okay, maybe I was exaggerating. It wasn't

as chaotic as it seemed. We had written out a rough order of events, which Stacey calmly began reading aloud. And the yard was beginning to look fantastic. Mallory and Claudia had made these cool signs, each showing a word in bold, comic-book-style neon letters. OUTRAGEOUS and DEATH-DEFYING were already hung, and Claudia was putting up STUPENDIST and HARE-RAISING.

I could see Mallory whispering something gently into Claudia's ear. Claudia looked crushed. (But hey, that's what rehearsals are for, right?) Claud began to take down those last two signs.

Now Vanessa was approaching me with this anxious expression on her face. "Kristy, what happens if you don't match the world's record? Do you have to keep repeating the event until you do?"

"It's just a demonstration," I patiently explained.

"But what if you do break it? The book will already be finished!"

"We'll do another printing," I said. "It's a living book."

Vanessa scampered back to the other kids. "Yyyyyyes!"

"Living book?" muttered Stacey.

"Yeah, I just made that up," I replied. "Sounds good, huh?"

She let out a guffaw and went back to work. (Like I said, I get no respect.)

Jessi came bounding out the door. She'd been inside, at the Spiers' kitchen table, writing invitations to the show. "How do you spell Ohdner?" she asked.

Mary Anne called out the answer.

"Don't you have the BSC record book in there?" I asked.

"Yup." Jessi shrugged. "It just didn't look right."

"I can spell Prezzioso!" Jenny chimed in. "P-R-E — "

All at once, all the kids began spelling their names aloud.

And another event was born — speed-spelling!

At this rate, we were on track for a record of our own: World's Longest World's Record Show.

The truth? I didn't want the rehearsal to end. Because afterward I had a much tougher project.

I had vowed to call Bart that night.

No, I had not done it yet. Yes, three days had passed since I'd talked to Mary Anne about it.

"Zounds!" you may be saying. Or maybe

"Gadzooks!" Kristy Thomas, too chicken to call Bart Taylor?

Cluck, cluck, cluck, cluck.

What can I say? I tried to call Bart four times on Sunday. But each time, I hung up before the call went through. I could feel myself clam up. I was afraid I'd open my mouth and say "Abbadabbadabba."

So Sunday night I called Mary Anne again, and she suggested writing everything down in advance. Which, of course, took the rest of the evening.

I was all set to call him Monday, until I read what I'd written. I decided to revise it.

Now, on Tuesday, it was time. No more beating around the bush. Like it or not, Bart was a part of my life. He was surely going to be at the show. And he had asked me to the April Fools' Day Dance the next week. I had to let him know where I stood.

I took out my speech and set it by the phone. Then I gritted my teeth and called.

"Hello?"

Bart's voice. My teeth felt glued together. Which was probably the only reason my heart didn't jump right out of my mouth.

"Who's this?" Bart said.

I picked up my speech and read aloud:

" 'Hi, Bart, how's it going?' "

"Kristy? Hi!" The *hi* was more a squeak than a word. He cleared his throat and tried again. "I mean, hi. Listen, I'm sorry. I don't know what I said to upset you, but I didn't mean to — "

" 'I realize I hung up on you and that was rude,' " I read.

"That's okay. I'm just not sure I — "

" 'So I would like to clarify my position in terms of my feelings and in regard to the breakage of the house rule which you already know about. First of all, I have and will like you in the sense of being a friend, but I felt that the pressure which I was feeling from you was changing the way that I conceived of our friendship but maybe not in the direction that it was meant to happen in my own mind, and not in the sense of measuring up to what you expected in terms of me being a girlfriend or not.' "

There. I had said it.

Bart didn't respond for awhile. I let my words hang for a moment, let him weigh it all out, catch the full impact.

"Kristy," he finally said, "could you run that by me again?"

"Ba-art!" I cried.

"Well, it sounded as if you were reading from a textbook or something. I'm not sure what you said."

116

So much for writing my feelings out. I let the paper fall to the floor. "What I meant was, I had some time to think about what happened. I'm not mad at you anymore, Bart. I know you didn't mean to cause trouble. I mean, you want me to be your girlfriend, and that's not so bad. You're a great guy and all, and I'm glad you like me so much. And I like you, too, really. Just not the same way."

"Well, how *do* you like me?" Bart asked.

"Look, I'm not ready to be what you want me to be, that's all," I pushed on. "I know it sounds weird, because we've been going out and kissing and stuff, but I always thought of us as just buds. Pals. That's why it didn't even occur to me that I was doing something wrong that night."

"So you want to — "

"It's just that different people mature at different rates," I quickly continued. "Sort of like learning to walk. Some do it at nine months, some at fifteen. You just can't push certain things. I was feeling pushed by you. First I was angry at you, and then I was angry at myself for not seeing what was happening between us. Now I do see. Anyway, Bart Man, everything's cool. I'm not saying I don't want to see you or I hate you. I just want things to stay on the friend level, that's all. Okay? Oh, and Bart?"

"Uh-huh?"

"I have a lot of stuff to do for the show this week. At school tomorrow, can you give Shannon the *Record Wreckers* sheets you have, so she can bring them to the BSC meeting?"

"Uh, sure. But — "

"Thanks, Bart Man. I'm glad we had the chance to talk. See you at the show."

Click.

The moment I hung up, I felt as if a sack of cement had been lifted from my shoulders.

Finally, things with Bart could return to normal.

CHAPTER 14

"Is everybody ready?" Mary Anne asked.

She had gathered us in her kitchen for brunch. It was Saturday morning, and the show was to begin at noon, which was only two hours away.

The week had been crazy. We'd had another rehearsal on Thursday, but during it, so many kids broke existing records that *all* the participants wanted to set new records.

I enjoyed the bustle, though. I was in such a great mood now that Bart and I had worked things out.

Bart, by the way, had handed his record sheets to Shannon at Stoneybrook Day School. Shannon had given them to Mary Anne, who had carefully collated them with the others. All week long she had slaved away at the final version of the *Record Wreckers* book, using all kinds of fancy computer software.

Up until Saturday, though, none of the rest of us had seen it.

We watched as Mary Anne set a cardboard box on the table and opened it.

Inside was a humongous book. On the cover, gold-stenciled letters spelled out *Record Wreckers: The BSC Book of Kids' Wild, Wacko, Off-the-Wall Records*. "Ta-da!" Mary Anne sang.

"Who-o-o-oa!" Stacey gasped.

"It's so cool!" gushed Claudia.

"Unbelievable!" added Jessi.

Shannon, Logan, Mallory, and Abby all put in their oohs and aahs.

"What do you think, Kristy?" Mary Anne asked.

"Nice," I said.

Mary Anne looked concerned. "Is something wrong?"

I shrugged. "I just thought it was supposed to be the *Thomas* book of records."

"Aauuugh!" Abby groaned.

Claudia beaned me with a chocolate croissant.

I have to admit, it really was gorgeous. Basically it was a fancy photo album, with removable cardboard three-hole pages, each hole bound with a little bendable brass thingy. Each page was covered with a plastic protector that a paper sheet could be slipped into.

The sheets themselves listed the records in all kinds of bold fonts, with crazy little computer pictures around the edges — a locomotive for the Brio train race, a singing face for the speed-singing event, stuff like that.

"I love it!" I said with a grin. "Really. Now let's get to work!"

We finished our brunch and went outside. It was chilly and damp, so we'd decided to hold most of the show in the barn.

Claudia and Mallory began hanging the banners. Mary Anne and Jessi brought folding chairs out of the Spiers' basement, and Abby and I set them up. Shannon and Logan cleared away junk, and Stacey swept.

The first people to arrive were the Barrett/DeWitts. They are a blended family of seven kids, five of whom had set some records when Abby sat for them.

"I brought my pogo stick!" Buddy announced.

"No, *I* brought your pogo stick," said his stepdad, lugging a contraption the size of a jackhammer.

"I have my dead fly collection!" Lindsey called out.

That must have been a new event. I didn't ask.

By eleven forty-five, the barn was full.

Claudia and Mallory's banners looked, well . . . SENSATIONAL, COLOSSAL, and PHENOMINAL!

(Oops. Nothing's perfect.)

I was working like crazy, cramming people in, answering questions from the kids, organizing props, dealing with emergencies.

Several emergencies.

On a dare from Linny, Nicky Pike took a bite out of a raw potato, and barfed up his breakfast. Jamie Newton started unrolling the toilet paper that Matt was supposed to use for his skateboard event. Someone sat on Margo's bananas, making them unpeelable (Mr. Spier ran out to buy more). Byron's Cap'n Crunch box ended up in the greedy hands of David Michael. And Margo's hats fell into a puddle.

While most of this chaos was going on, I was in the yard, setting up the outdoor events. I was coaching Linny on the backward jump when I spotted Bart. He was biking up the road, waving to me. His friends Seth and Kevin were riding alongside him.

I waved back. My stomach fluttered a little, but I was pretty cool and collected. What a difference from a few days earlier.

As Bart parked his bike, Linny, Hannie, Bill, and Melody surrounded him. Jabbering away, they pulled him toward the barn.

He smiled at me, shrugged, and walked into the barn with them. Bart's friends trudged along behind him.

At ten minutes to twelve, I hustled all the participants into the barn. Mary Anne had set up an on-deck area under the hayloft. She was standing there with the order of events on a clipboard. The other BSC members were busy herding kids, breaking up fights, tying shoes, and all the other normal stuff.

I had written out a speech and put it in my pocket. But I thought about my phone conversation with Bart and decided I was better shooting from the hip.

I grabbed my bullhorn, which was hanging on a hook inside the door. "Attention, everyone!" I called out. "Please take your seats."

The crowd shuffled around and sat. Well, most of them. Along the back wall was a group of standees, including Watson and Mom.

Charlie and his girlfriend, Sarah, sat in the front row, gazing up at me.

"Ladies and gentlemen and children and all clients and charges of the Baby-sitters Club!" I began.

I could see Sarah taking Charlie's hand and squeezing it. She smiled at him and rested her head on his shoulder.

I don't know why this flustered me, but it

did. "Relcome to *Weckers Record*," I began. "It's a demonstration of power, agility . . . um, ability, creativity, and . . ."

I couldn't think of the word.

I fished around in my pocket for the speech. Someone in the crowd yawned.

I took the speech out, unfolded it, and said, "Hijinks!"

Everyone laughed. Including Charlie and Sarah. And my parents. And Bart.

" 'So be prepared for the show of a lifetime, for events you never dreamed possible,' " I read. " 'And all brought to you by the Baby-sitters Club, serving the greater Stoneybrook community and meeting every Monday, Wednesday, and Friday from five-thirty to six, at — ' "

"Kristyyyyy!" Claudia hissed.

I quickly gave our phone number and let the show begin.

First Byron demonstrated the Cap'n Crunch toss. He managed ten in a row and received a big ovation.

The next scheduled event was Jenny's speed-singing. She was going to perform "I've Been Working on the Railroad." But when Mary Anne gently nudged her toward the stage, she froze.

"Go on, honey," Mrs. P. said, rising from her seat.

124

Jenny jumped into her mom's arms. Together they walked center stage.

"IIIII've been working — " Mrs. P. began to sing.

"*Noooooooo!*" Jenny shrieked, burying her head in her mom's shoulder.

"I'll do it!" Claire shouted from the sidelines. "I've been — "

Jenny spun around, glaring at her. "*I'VE-BEENWORKINGONTHERAILROADALLTHE-LIVELONGDAYI'VEBEEN . . .*"

Both girls raced to the end, and the crowd went wild.

"I won!" Jenny boasted.

"No, I did!" Claire retorted.

"It's a demonstration, not a competition," I reminded them.

Next Karen and David Michael did the egg catch. With each toss, the audience would let out a "Whoa!" that became louder and louder until David Michael cracked up.

And because he did, so did the egg.

Have no fear, Kristy's cleanup crew was in fine form. (Thank goodness the eggs were hard-boiled.)

The audience members were really in the spirit. They applauded for David Michael's world's longest burp (although Mom turned beet red). They patiently counted aloud as Buddy jumped ninety-seven times on his pogo stick. For "There Was an Old Lady," the entire audience answered each disgusting verse with a loud "Ewww" that delighted the singers, right up to "There was an old lady who swallowed the universe; What a curse to swallow the universe . . ."

And no one gagged when Lindsey DeWitt showed how many dead flies she could fit on a Post-It note. Unfortunately, as she was holding it up to wild applause, Andrew walked out to do his World's Most Realistic Sneeze and sprayed the bugs all over the front two rows. (Poor Sarah and Charlie.)

Halfway through the show, two-year-old Marnie Barrett became hungry and started crying. Luckily for us, Margo the barefoot banana-peeler was able to work Marnie into the act, giving direct foot-to-mouth service. (Gross, I know, but Marnie didn't seem to mind.)

The final verdict? Well, the response from the crowd is always the best indicator.

"YEEEEEEEAAAAAAAA!" (Something like that.)

We were a hit. The kids took so many bows, they looked as if they were bobbing for apples.

When the BSC joined hands onstage, I made Bart share our bow with us.

He took my hand. As we bowed, I smiled at him. He smiled back.

Afterward, the kids were beside themselves, running around, congratulating each other, congratulating themselves. Jenny the reluctant performer was singing up a storm. Matt was trying to break Linny's backward jump record. The rest of the kids were passing the book around, finding their names in it.

While the audience cleared out, Mary Anne and Abby began sweeping up Cap'n Crunch nuggets, dead flies, and all the other debris. I wanted to help them, but I needed to do something else first.

Bart was by his bike, putting on his helmet. Kevin and Seth were already on their bikes, making wide circles in the street.

"Hi," I greeted Bart.

"Great show, Kristy," he said. "But you didn't have to let me bow like that."

"You deserved it," I replied.

Bart smiled. "Thanks. Well, I guess I'll see you."

"You know, Bart, I was really happy you were here."

"Yeah," Bart said softly. "Me, too."

"Now that the weather's nicer, let's schedule a game between the Krushers and the Bashers, okay?"

"You bet." Bart swung his leg over his bike.

"Okay, well, see you next week. Make sure to wear your dancing shoes!"

Bart was about to pedal away but he didn't. "Huh?"

"You know, the April Fools' Day Dance?" I reminded him. "At your school? Did you forget?"

"Well, no," Bart replied. "But we're not going to that dance together."

"I thought — didn't you ask — we're friends again, aren't we?"

"Sure we are. But this is a *dance*, Kristy. I don't want to take just a friend to the dance."

"Yo, Bart, are we leaving or what?" called Kevin.

"Okay!" Bart shouted. As he hopped on his bike and rolled away, he said, "See you, Kristy."

I may have answered. I'm not sure, though. Chances are I was too busy scraping my pride off the sidewalk.

"I don't care!" I paced up and down Mary Anne's bedroom floor. "He's a creep!"

"Look, Kristy, I know you're upset," Mary Anne said. "But this is what you wanted, right?"

"What, to be rejected?" I snapped. "Thrown away like a . . . a used plastic diaper?"

"Gag me, Kristy," Stacey remarked.

"That would have been an interesting event," Claud added.

I wheeled around at them. "Can't you guys take anything seriously?"

I know. I was being unfair. After all, the show had ended an hour ago, and my friends had stuck around to help me out.

"What I meant was, when you talked to him on the phone, you said you wanted him to be just a friend, right?" Mary Anne asked.

"Of course!" I said.

"And *he* said okay?" Claudia asked.

"Yes," I replied. "I think."

"What do you mean, you think?" Stacey said.

"I don't remember!"

Mary Anne looked puzzled. "But he agreed he'd take you to the dance?"

"No. We didn't talk about that."

"What *did* he say, Kristy?" Claudia asked.

I shrugged. "Not much. I guess I did most of the talking."

"Wait. Let me get this straight," Stacey said. "You broke up with him. You said, 'Let's be friends.' He asked someone else to the dance. And you're surprised?"

"Who did he ask to the dance?" The words just flew out of my mouth.

"I don't know!" Stacey shot back. "I'm just repeating what you said."

"I didn't say he was taking someone else!" I said. "Is he? I mean, did he say something to any of you?"

Claudia shook her head. "Kristy, I don't believe you. So what if he does? Hey, you're my friend, and I don't get bent out of shape if you don't take me to a dance."

"Claudia, that's different," I said.

"Why?" Stacey asked. "Because he's a boy?"

"Yeah," I replied.

"So you *do* want to be his girlfriend," Mary Anne said.

"No!" I closed my eyes and took a few deep breaths. I felt like Dorothy in *The Wizard of Oz*, spinning above Kansas in the cyclone. "I guess I'm just insulted or something. I mean, we used to go to dances before this. We didn't have to be officially boyfriend-girlfriend. And all I want is for us to go back to the way we were before."

Mary Anne nodded. "Yeah, but things change. Bart cares about you, in a much different way than you care about him."

"Then why does he have to go and hurt my feelings?"

"Did you ever consider that you may have hurt his feelings?" Stacey asked.

I'd been on the verge of railing about something, but I swallowed my words.

How could I be so stupid?

I'd forgiven him. I'd understood that he hadn't wanted to cause me any trouble, that he'd cared about me.

But I'd been so worried about what *I* was going to say, how *I* would express my tangled-up emotions, that I hadn't stopped to listen to him. To think about his feelings.

I tried to. It wasn't easy to imagine being in his shoes. But when I did, one thing became clear: If he did care about me, and I broke up with him, of course he'd be hurt.

Way to go, Kristy.

Oh, boy. I had really blown it.

I needed to talk to Bart, and soon.

After I biked home, I called Bart. He seemed surprised to hear my voice, but his friends were about to leave, and he agreed to go for a bike ride.

We rode along the outskirts of Stoneybrook. Crocuses were peeking up between the trees, and you could see the occasional flash of a bluejay.

At first we didn't talk about much. When we finally exhausted the weather and the upcoming baseball season, I said, "Bart, I don't know if you noticed, but I was upset about not being invited to the dance."

"Notice?" Bart replied. "You looked like you wanted to kill me."

I laughed. "I'm sorry. I must seem pretty confusing, huh?"

"Well, up until then I wasn't confused at all. I mean, you did tell me how you felt."

"How do *you* feel, Bart?"

He shrugged. "Fine."

"I mean, about me. Us. I never asked you."

"Well, I guess I'm not, like, overjoyed or

anything. I was kind of thinking I was your . . . you know . . ."

"Boyfriend?"

"Whatever. Yeah." Bart exhaled loudly. "I don't know what happened. It's like, at first we were friends, buds, playing ball, goofing around. Okay, we went out and danced and kissed and stuff, but that was mainly because you're a girl and I'm a guy and that's the way it goes, no big deal. But then things changed. I didn't mean for it to happen, it just did."

"What happened?"

"You were different. Or maybe I was different. All I know is the kissing and dating didn't just feel like stuff we did because that's the way it goes. It was, like, the main thing. It was something I really wanted to do with you more than anything else." Bart snorted a laugh. "This doesn't make any sense, does it? You don't want to hear this."

"Yes, I do. Really."

"I like you, Kristy. A lot. You want us just to be friends, and hey, that's cool. I want to stay your friend. But it's going to take me awhile to adjust. You asked me how I feel? Well, I know it sounds stupid, but this whole thing makes me kind of lonely."

"You know," I said, "you don't have to feel lonely. If you want, I'll still go to that dance with you. The way we used to."

Bart shook his head. "I asked another girl, from my school."

"Oh."

"When you broke up with me, I just assumed you didn't want to go."

"But after the show, you said you didn't want to go to the party with just a friend," I reminded him. "Does that mean . . . ?"

Bart shook his head. "I just said that. I guess I was kind of mad and confused. I don't know her that well. She's nice, though. You'd like her."

"Oh. Good."

"You're not angry, are you?"

"No." I smiled. "Why should I be?"

We rode on awhile longer, not saying much. Then Bart challenged me to a race and I really whupped him.

Later on we had some hot chocolate at my house and planned our first Krusher–Basher game. We joked about our teams. We had a few laughs.

All in all, it was just the way it used to be.

Only different.

I don't know how the dance went. I never did talk to Bart about it. And I never saw him with the girl he took. She didn't come to games or walk home from school with him, and

Shannon hardly ever saw them together at Stoneybrook Day.

So maybe it didn't work out.

Or maybe it did. Anyway, it wasn't really my business.

Nowadays Bart and I are still buds. We see each other in the neighborhood. We argue with each other at games. We take our teams out for ice cream sometimes. But we don't talk on the phone as much as we used to. Or get together for catch and hitting practice. And we never go to the movies.

So in the end, everything worked out fine. When I do go to movies, I can face forward and see the whole film now. And when I'm sitting at home, I don't have to worry about Bart showing up unexpectedly.

But I have to admit, when I see Charlie and Sarah together, I get this funny feeling in my stomach. I don't really understand it, but it doesn't matter. After awhile, it goes away.

And so do my thoughts of Bart. More or less.

Dear Reader,

Kristy + Bart = ? is about a confusing time in Kristy's life, a time when she's faced with decisions she's not ready to make. A lot of kids have written to me to say that they feel pressured to have a boyfriend, or to be in a relationship they don't feel ready for. I wanted to address this issue in a BSC book, and felt that Kristy was the most likely character to find herself in this situation. Eventually, Kristy is mature enough to realize that people are ready for different things at different times. And just because her friends have boyfriends doesn't mean that she's ready for such a relationship right now. Fortunately, Kristy can rely on her friends to support her — and that's what friends are for.

Happy reading,

Ann M Martin

Ann M. Martin

L. GODWIN

About the Author

ANN MATTHEWS MARTIN was born on August 12, 1955. She grew up in Princeton, NJ, with her parents and her younger sister, Jane.

Although Ann used to be a teacher and then an editor of children's books, she's now a full-time writer. She gets the ideas for her books from many different places. Some are based on personal experiences. Others are based on childhood memories and feelings. Many are written about contemporary problems or events.

All of Ann's characters, even the members of the Baby-sitters Club, are made up. (So is Stoneybrook.) But many of her characters are based on real people. Sometimes Ann names her characters after people she knows, other times she chooses names she likes.

In addition to the Baby-sitters Club books, Ann Martin has written many other books for children. Her favorite is *Ten Kids, No Pets* because she loves big families and she loves animals. Her favorite Baby-sitters Club book is *Kristy's Big Day*. (By the way, Kristy is her favorite baby-sitter!)

Ann M. Martin now lives in New York with her cats, Gussie and Woody. Her hobbies are reading, sewing, and needlework — especially making clothes for children.

Notebook Pages

This Baby-sitters Club book belongs to _____ .

I am _____ years old and in the _____

grade.

The name of my school is _____ .

I got this BSC book from _____ .

I started reading it on _____ and

finished reading it on _____ .

The place where I read most of this book is _____ .

My favorite part was when _____ .

If I could change anything in the story, it might be the part when

_____ .

My favorite character in the Baby-sitters Club is _____ .

The BSC member I am most like is _____

because _____ .

If I could write a Baby-sitters Club book it would be about ____

_____ .

#95 Kristy + Bart = ?

In *Kristy + Bart = ?*, Kristy and Bart have problems because Bart wants Kristy to be a more serious girlfriend than she wants to be. One person who's liked me more than I've liked him/her is __ _____ . This is what happened: _____ _____ . A boy/girl I like is _____ . Kristy and Bart do not work out as boyfriend and girlfriend, while Mary Anne and Logan enjoy being a couple. This is what I think about boyfriends and girlfriends: _____ _____ . Two of my friends who should be boyfriend and girlfriend are _____ ____ and _____ . Two of my friends who should not be boyfriend and girlfriend are _____ and _____ . In the Baby-sitters Club, there have been many couples and "sort-of couples": Kristy and Bart; Mary Anne and Logan; Mallory and Ben; Stacey and Robert; and Jessi and Quint. The couple I like the most is: _____ _____ .

KRISTY'S

Playing softball with some of my favorite sitting charges.

A gab-fest

Me, age 3. Already on the go.

SCRAPBOOK

My family keeps growing!

with Mary Anne!

David Michael, me, and Louie — the best dog ever.

Illustrations by Angelo Tillery

Read all the books
about **Kristy**
in the Baby-sitters Club series
by Ann M. Martin

Look for #96

ABBY'S LUCKY THIRTEEN

The day after the test Anna said, "Are you okay, Abby?"

"I'm fine."

"You sure?"

"Yes! Why are you picking on me?"

Anna looked surprised and a little hurt. "I'm not picking on you. You just looked — hassled."

I smiled a little at that. It was an old hippie word, one of the ones our father had used, sort of jokingly.

"I guess I am a little hassled," I admitted. I looked at my twin. Could I trust her? Could I pour out the whole horrible story and ask for her advice?

I took a deep breath. "I'm just worried about this Bat Mitzvah stuff. You know."

It wasn't a lie. It was just part of the truth, that was all.

Anna nodded. "It's starting to worry me

more and more. But you know what? That happens before performances, too. You sort of worry and worry and worry and just when you think you're going to go crazy, you get very calm. It's like, suddenly you've accepted your fate, or something. You know there's nothing you can do but do it." She grinned at me. "Like that commercial you like. About the athletic shoes."

"I'll be glad when that moment comes," I said. But my mind was already spinning off into other directions. To become a Bat Mitzvah meant to become an adult, with an adult's responsibilities. Didn't that include telling the truth? Like about what had happened with the math test?

Maybe it wasn't even legal for me to become a Bat Mitzvah after something like this had happened.

We went into our separate bedrooms and I pulled out the book Rabbi Dorman had lent me.

Rabbi Dorman. For a moment, I considered talking to him. But I pushed the thought away.

And I studied my Torah portion.

With a guilty conscience.

THE BABY-SITTERS Club ®

by Ann M. Martin

More titles... ▶

The Baby-sitters Club titles continued...

❑ MG47011-6	#73 Mary Anne and Miss Priss	$3.50
❑ MG47012-4	#74 Kristy and the Copycat	$3.50
❑ MG47013-2	#75 Jessi's Horrible Prank	$3.50
❑ MG47014-0	#76 Stacey's Lie	$3.50
❑ MG48221-1	#77 Dawn and Whitney, Friends Forever	$3.50
❑ MG48222-X	#78 Claudia and Crazy Peaches	$3.50
❑ MG48223-8	#79 Mary Anne Breaks the Rules	$3.50
❑ MG48224-6	#80 Mallory Pike, #1 Fan	$3.50
❑ MG48225-4	#81 Kristy and Mr. Mom	$3.50
❑ MG48226-2	#82 Jessi and the Troublemaker	$3.50
❑ MG48235-1	#83 Stacey vs. the BSC	$3.50
❑ MG48228-9	#84 Dawn and the School Spirit War	$3.50
❑ MG48236-X	#85 Claudi Kishi, Live from WSTO	$3.50
❑ MG48227-0	#86 Mary Anne and Camp BSC	$3.50
❑ MG48237-8	#87 Stacey and the Bad Girls	$3.50
❑ MG22872-2	#88 Farewell, Dawn	$3.50
❑ MG22873-0	#89 Kristy and the Dirty Diapers	$3.50
❑ MG45575-3	Logan's Story Special Edition Readers' Request	$3.25
❑ MG47118-X	Logan Bruno, Boy Baby-sitter Special Edition Readers' Request	$3.50
❑ MG47756-0	Shannon's Story Special Edition	$3.50
❑ MG44240-6	Baby-sitters on Board! Super Special #1	$3.95
❑ MG44239-2	Baby-sitters' Summer Vacation Super Special #2	$3.95
❑ MG43973-1	Baby-sitters' Winter Vacation Super Special #3	$3.95
❑ MG42493-9	Baby-sitters' Island Adventure Super Special #4	$3.95
❑ MG43575-2	California Girls! Super Special #5	$3.95
❑ MG43576-0	New York, New York! Super Special #6	$3.95
❑ MG44963-X	Snowbound Super Special #7	$3.95
❑ MG44962-X	Baby-sitters at Shadow Lake Super Special #8	$3.95
❑ MG45661-X	Starring the Baby-sitters Club Super Special #9	$3.95
❑ MG45674-1	Sea City, Here We Come! Super Special #10	$3.95
❑ MG47015-9	The Baby-sitter's Remember Super Special #11	$3.95
❑ MG48308-0	Here Come the Bridesmaids Super Special #12	$3.95

Available wherever you buy books...or use this order form.

Scholastic Inc., P.O. Box 7502, 2931 E. McCarty Street, Jefferson City, MO 65102

Please send me the books I have checked above. I am enclosing $ _____
(please add $2.00 to cover shipping and handling). Send check or money order—no cash or C.O.D.s please.

Name _____ Birthdate _____

Address _____

City _____ State/Zip _____

Please allow four to six weeks for delivery. Offer good in the U.S. only. Sorry, mail orders are not available to residents of Canada. Prices subject to change.

ALL NEW!

by Ann M. Martin

Meet the best friends you'll ever have!

Have you heard? The BSC has a new look
—and more great stuff than ever before.
An all-new scrapbook for each book's narrator!
A letter from Ann M. Martin! Fill-in pages to
personalize your copy! Order today!

❏ BBD22473-5	#1	**Kristy's Great Idea**	$3.50
❏ BBD22763-7	#2	**Claudia and the Phantom Phone Calls**	$3.99
❏ BBD25158-9	#3	**The Truth About Stacey**	$3.99
❏ BBD25159-7	#4	**Mary Anne Saves the Day**	$3.50
❏ BBD25160-0	#5	**Dawn and the Impossible Three**	$3.50
❏ BBD25161-9	#6	**Kristy's Big Day**	$3.50
❏ BBD25162-7	#7	**Claudia and Mean Janine**	$3.50
❏ BBD25163-5	#8	**Boy Crazy Stacey**	$3.50
❏ BBD25164-3	#9	**The Ghost at Dawn's House**	$3.99
❏ BBD25165-1	#10	**Logan Likes Mary Anne!**	$3.99
❏ BBD25166-X	#11	**Kristy and the Snobs**	$3.99
❏ BBD25167-8	#12	**Claudia and the New Girl**	$3.99

Available wherever you buy books, or use this order form.

THE BABY-SITTERS CLUB®

by Ann M. Martin

Collect and read these exciting BSC Super Specials, Mysteries, and Super Mysteries along with your favorite Baby-sitters Club books!

BSC Super Specials

❑ BBK44240-6	Baby-sitters on Board! Super Special #1	$3.95
❑ BBK44239-2	Baby-sitters' Summer Vacation Super Special #2	$3.95
❑ BBK43973-1	Baby-sitters' Winter Vacation Super Special #3	$3.95
❑ BBK42493-9	Baby-sitters' Island Adventure Super Special #4	$3.95
❑ BBK43575-2	California Girls! Super Special #5	$3.95
❑ BBK43576-0	New York, New York! Super Special #6	$3.95
❑ BBK44963-X	Snowbound! Super Special #7	$3.95
❑ BBK44962-X	Baby-sitters at Shadow Lake Super Special #8	$3.95
❑ BBK45661-X	Starring The Baby-sitters Club! Super Special #9	$3.95
❑ BBK45674-1	Sea City, Here We Come! Super Special #10	$3.95
❑ BBK47015-9	The Baby-sitters Remember Super Special #11	$3.95
❑ BBK48308-0	Here Come the Bridesmaids! Super Special #12	$3.95

BSC Mysteries

❑ BAI44084-5	#1 Stacey and the Missing Ring	$3.50
❑ BAI44085-3	#2 Beware Dawn!	$3.50
❑ BAI44799-8	#3 Mallory and the Ghost Cat	$3.50
❑ BAI44800-5	#4 Kristy and the Missing Child	$3.50
❑ BAI44801-3	#5 Mary Anne and the Secret in the Attic	$3.50
❑ BAI44961-3	#6 The Mystery at Claudia's House	$3.50
❑ BAI44960-5	#7 Dawn and the Disappearing Dogs	$3.50
❑ BAI44959-1	#8 Jessi and the Jewel Thieves	$3.50
❑ BAI44958-3	#9 Kristy and the Haunted Mansion	$3.50

More titles ➡

The Baby-sitters Club books continued...

BSC Super Mysteries

Available wherever you buy books...or use this order form.

Scholastic Inc., P.O. Box 7502, 2931 East McCarty Street, Jefferson City, MO 65102-7502

Please send me the books I have checked above. I am enclosing $ _____
(please add $2.00 to cover shipping and handling). Send check or money order
— no cash or C.O.D.s please.

Name_____Birthdate_____

Address _____

City_____State/Zip_____

Please allow four to six weeks for delivery. Offer good in the U.S. only. Sorry, mail orders are not available to residents of Canada. Prices subject to change.

BSCM795

What's the scoop with Dawn, Kristy, Mallory, and the other girls?

Be the first to know with G★I★R★L★ magazine!

Hey, Baby-sitters Club readers! Now you can be the first on the block to get in on the action of G★I★R★L★ It's an exciting new magazine that lets you dig in and read...

★ Upcoming selections from Ann Martin's Baby-sitters Club books
★ Fun articles on handling stress, turning dreams into great careers, making and keeping best friends, and much more
★ Plus, all the latest on new movies, books, music, and sports!

To get in on the scoop, just cut and mail this coupon today. And don't forget to tell all your friends about G★I★R★L★ magazine!

A neat offer for you...6 issues for only $15.00.